Blue

WILLOW BIRCH

ISBN-10:1508680418
ISBN-13: 978-1508680413

CONTENTS

ACKNOWLEDGMENTS

I should like to thank my husband for providing cover artwork, but also for proofreading the text while naively failing to understand barely a word of it. I also should like to thank my friend and critique reader who diligently proofread the text (while successfully hiding it from her husband).

None of the characters in this book are based on real people, so any resemblances that you may find to persons living or dead are entirely the product of your own naughty imagination.

1 ARRIVAL OF THE NEW BOY

"Blue – Personal Services. How can I help you?" I purred in my most seductive come-to-bed telephone voice. "Certainly sir, a booking for 7pm tonight?"...."Yes we have a range of services. Whatever your preferences. Straight vanilla or full on BDSM, Submissive or Dominant. We also have a range of fantasy themes: Schoolmistress; Gymkhana ponies; Mummy and baby; or "Plushies" in a selection of animals. We also have our "Fairy story" menu, with Goldilocks; Little Red Riding Hood; or Bo Peep, with inflatable or plushy sheep."

Why do telephones sit there silently for hours, then they all start ringing at once? Sometimes I really could do with a bit of a hand around here with the admin side of the business. I deftly selected the option for hold on the red coloured telephone, picking up the black handset in its place. "Could you hold the line for just one moment while I check the ladies for their availability?" *Now to get rid of that Old Dear...*

Transforming my tone now (at least as best that I could approximate), to reflect polite but sharp, business-like efficiency, I switched myself seamlessly, back into the role of "Harriet Harrison", Police civilian administrative officer. "Yes, Mrs Wilson, it seems that we already have little Bobby here." "He was brought in to the counter just a few moments ago," glancing up at the monitor display of the counter area, where an elderly gentleman was vainly attempting to unravel the lead of a small Yorkshire terrier, which

1

was successfully defeating his best efforts by weaving itself in and out of his ankles.

Give the old girl a break, why don't you...
"Of course we will keep him here until you can come for him...No. It's no bother at all. I shall pass on your message that he's been a very naughty boy again....See you soon".

Replacing the black handset, substituting it once more with the red coloured one, and flicking the hold button again to release, I broke back into my attempt at a sultry purr without a second's hesitation, "No problem at all Dr Sinclair, Lady Sabrina will be able to attend to all of your needs tonight. Shall I just put it down for one of our "Taster" sessions, so you can decide on your selection when you get here?...Wonderful... Look forward to seeing you later."

As I glanced around at the ordered confusion I call my office, with my haphazardly stacked trays of paper work; my eyes followed the spaghetti of wires winding up the back of my battered old desk, leading to the two telephones: one black for Police use; one red – my "business" hotline. The paintwork was old, in need of refreshment (much like everything else around here), giving a bleak "minimalist" appearance, all the more so for the battered, meagre office furniture; an old, battered grey metal filing cabinet leaning crookedly against one wall; an equally battered tall, grey metal double-doored cupboard in the corner. *If only they knew what I keep in that cupboard.* The thought tickled me somehow.

The Station was typical of those which might be found in many regional small towns. It was a late Victorian-style red brick building with two floors; the upper floor in the shiny, hard Accrington brick, common to older-style higher-status buildings in the northern counties; the ground floor faced with an outer sheath of decorative white rendering, to provide a low-budget impression of Portland stone. It had endured many years of weathering from the salty, seaside air; along with the rigours of modern-day traffic pollutants. The surface, despite a half-hearted attempt at some low-budget cosmetic cleansing some decades previously, was also tarnished by a century-deep layer of carbon pumped out from the neighbouring railway station (the height of Westhaven-on-Sea's now diminished popularity as a seaside resort, coinciding with the glorious days of steam).

The exterior of the building reflected the overall condition in general. Once the pride of the town, it had seen little by way of maintenance for many years, other than the very basic "modernisations" of the installation of electric lighting (which in itself speaks volumes for the decades of neglect). The out-dated and peeling state of the interior decoration was just a minor outward manifestation of the overall state of the crumbling infrastructure beneath. The entire building was in need of a serious input of resources devoted to refurbishment which the annually decreasing budget did not provide. At least our little hobby turned business project had eased the burden slightly, and had even provided funds to fix up a few areas that were looking particularly jaded. This office though was sadly in need of a bit of TLC in the near future. If nothing else, at least it was a bit warmer in here this year than it used to be. It used to be like asking Mr Scrooge for another piece of coal for the fire, trying to get the "Super" to raise the thermostat by just a degree.

Glancing absent-mindedly past the tattered, off-white fabric strips of the vertical blinds, through the layers of grimy sea salt coating the office window, my eyes were drawn to a solitary figure venturing across the early February frost on the car park below. He made me feel cold just to look at him. Then I remembered. It must be the new rookie Police constable, fresh from the academy, arriving for his first day at the station. I'd forgotten that he was due today.

On closer examination he looked young and fresh faced (younger than the 24 years that it had said in his file anyway), of about average height (looked to be about 5'8"); skinny, with mousy blonde, short cropped hair. *The body could do with some work, but there is potential. Yes, I could definitely do something with that. In fact it might just be fun, making something of him. Someone new to train. A chance for a little "instruction".*

* * *

This was going to be my first posting at a real working station since my graduation from the Academy and it was with great trepidation that I stepped off the safety of the pavement and committed myself to that walk across the car park. That's it now. No going back around the block again and hoping that nobody had seen me (I was still hoping that nobody saw me the first time, when I did chicken out and go around the block once more). The ground would be frosty this morning too, making loud crunching noises with every step I took on the gravel. As I stepped inside, the welcoming warmth of the building hit me. It was a pleasant contrast to the freezing morning air outside. That was definitely Brass Monkey weather out there.

The counter area certainly matched the outside: battered paintwork, peeling walls, the linoleum floor cracked and chipped, with pale patches where the colour of its pattern had been bleached away by the vomit of uncountable years of weekend drunks. In one corner of the room, an elderly gentleman was trying unsuccessfully to un-braid a dog leash from around his legs, in a failed attempt to remove a small, yapping and snapping ball of grey fur, which apart from the slavering teeth could easily be mistaken for a heavily soiled floor mop. The officer on counter duties, with his sour face, looked just about as miserable as the whole building. They matched well. He didn't look to be a barrel of laughs.

I approached the counter, but he ignored me, continuing to scribble in his notebook. I cleared my throat, shuffling nervously. *Try not to show any sign of weakness. He'll eat you for breakfast.* Again he ignored me, continuing with his scribbling. Eventually he stopped and I thought he must be ready, but no. Now he turned and started to rummage in the drawer to his right. I cleared my throat again, even louder this time. He slowly turned to face me, regarding me as though something infectious had just crawled in.

"Yes?"

"PC 3489 Titterington reporting sir," I answered as quietly as I could manage, hoping that nobody else had heard. *Why on earth did my father not change his name? Why did he land me with a*

4

name like "Titterington"? As if "Timothy" wasn't bad enough?

"Repeat?"

You've got to be having a laugh here now. Surely you heard me? You're just taking the piss!

I repeated, slightly louder this time, "PC 3489 Titterington reporting for duty"

"What was the name again?"

Almost shouting this time "TIT-TER-ING-TON!"

"You're late...and there's no need to shout. I heard you perfectly well the first time."

With that he slowly rose from his seat, crossing to the opposite end of the counter, where he pressed a buzzer releasing the doorway though into the main corridor.

"Through the main office, turn to your right, down the main corridor, 3rd door, ask for Harry, the Admin....she runs the place" he ordered briskly, then sat himself back down, picked up a newspaper lying on the counter next to him, and turned to page 3.

Puzzled to hear that a civilian admin was in charge, rather than a ranking officer, I shrugged off the thought for now (*things seem to be done a bit differently out here in the sticks*) and passed through the side door into a large room. From the look of it, this must be the main office. It was a large room, with faded, grimy pale blue painted plaster walls and chipped white paintwork. The only windows were on one wall, high up above head height, to prevent any kind of view of the car park. The glass was protected on the outside by a thick metal grill, which had obviously not been removed for many years judging on the thick layers of salty grime built up on the glass, obscuring most of whatever light it had originally afforded. There were a number of old, battered desks, lined up against the wall around the perimeter, some set up with computer terminals. A handful of equally battered rotating office chairs were positioned in front of these terminals, many with areas of dirty foam exposed, where they had long before lost their surface upholstery. On the walls were a number of printed photos of the town's current "most wanted" (on at least one of whom, some wag had chosen to draw a pair of glasses and a goatee beard); and just about every inch of desk surface was littered with a scattering of abandoned paperwork. Here and there equally abandoned coffee cups (with rather suspicious looking furry contents), sat atop piles of paperwork, as though serving as "organic" paperweights.

At the far side of the office was a door, presumably leading to the main corridor and the rest of the Station (presumably also leading to "Harry's office"). To the left were a set of double doors leading out of the Station into the side street. As I stood there taking in the disorganised chaos that passed as the main office, the double doors burst open, and through them stumbled a dishevelled and terrified looking teenager, closely followed by a portly looking Sergeant, clutching a transparent bag full of indeterminate but suspicious looking vegetable matter.

"Ah, you must be the new bloke then?" he greeted me. Throwing down the bag on the nearest desk, closely followed by his cap, he extended a hand "Toscer, 7865. Not been here that long myself. In the city branch for close on 20 years before that. Don't piss me off and we'll get on fine....Oh, and before you get any ideas, my name is pronounced TOZE-ER, not what those others around here will tell you"

Not exactly the friendliest greeting I'd ever experienced. Looking at him now, with his colourless, pale blue eyes, as nearly a twenty-year man, he was of an age when most officers would be looking to retirement. The fact that he had recently been transferred here to this small town station at this stage in his career, spoke volumes for the lack of esteem in which his former colleagues in the city must have held him. They probably transferred him to be rid of him, unable to stand for another second his arrogant, pompous attitude. No doubt it wouldn't be long until his new colleagues warmed similarly to him. Certainly I shouldn't be sorry to see him go.

I reckon the others have probably got it right if they've been calling him "Tosser" - it suits him.

Picking up the bag of confiscated organics and tossing it at me, he directed that I should give it to the mysterious "Harry", to put in the Evidence Room. He then added that he doesn't trust her and that I should "watch my step with her", also that I should tell him about anything I saw going on. It was all more than just a little mysterious. Then, with that he turned for the second door, "Come on then. Let's get shut of this one."

As he seemed to be heading in my direction anyway, and considering it best not to rub him up the wrong way too soon, I followed him and the hapless teen through the other door into the main corridor, turning right towards the first door on the right, marked "Custody Suite".

Decorated in much similar fashion to the rest of the Station, with crumbling pale blue painted plaster and battered white paintwork, the Custody Suite was also long overdue for a refurbishment. To one side it was fitted out with a tall, pine counter, too high for persons approaching to see over to the other side. On the opposite side, the floor level was raised, so that the counter height for the custody officer seated behind it was correctly at waist height, forcing any persons approaching to have to look up to him. Computer monitors were set obliquely into the inner edge of the counter, for ease of viewing by the user, without obscuring his or her view of those being brought in to be charged. On the wall behind the counter, a white board was set up with a grid, listing two interview rooms and each cell by number, date and time of admission, the name of its occupant, and the purpose for which they had been detained. To the right of the counter, a short corridor then led first to the two interview rooms, followed by the various cells as listed on the board.

Having handed over his prisoner to the officer in charge, Sergeant Toscer then wiped his hands of him and headed back out on patrol. However, from the ensuing conversation which I overheard between the Custody officer and his second in command, there were currently no spare cells - .a fact borne out by the wall chart behind him. There was only one cell currently in operation and it was occupied by an overnight drunk. To my surprise I heard him offering the boy some form of "alternative punishment". He suggested either washing the Judge's car for month (at the prospect of which the youngster's face visibly screwed up); or serving as delivery boy for the Women's Institute cakes ("Granny's Herbal Cakes" he called them). To my surprise he decided for the latter, although I had not thought that teenagers would have been even remotely interested in cakes really.

Fascinating as it was(n't) to be stood around discussing the niceties of confectionery delivery, time was creeping on, so I reckoned it was probably time I made my exit, so making my goodbyes to the Custody officer, I headed back off down the main corridor towards "Harry's office".

This is just about the strangest Police Station I have ever been in. It is nothing like they tell you in the Academy.

* * *

2 INTRODUCTIONS

The mysterious "Harry", who apparently runs the Station, looked nothing like I had been expecting. Certainly she was not on the force, but was civilian, so was not in uniform. Instead she was dressed in a smart, close fitting navy blue shirt dress, belted at the waist but with rather a more daringly plunging neckline than I would have expected for office wear. It certainly showed off her very well-endowed figure for the best of its attributes, clinging to her tall, yet muscular frame, and bringing out the colour of her soft olive skin. She had dark brown hair, short-cropped in an elfin style, with dark brown eyes and the longest lashes I had ever seen. It was hard to place an age on her. Certainly she was not young (but seemed young to be in the position of running the station), with a maturity that defined her as a "woman" rather than a "girl" – a few years older than I was definitely, but possibly not much more than 30. I couldn't help looking, but the goods definitely out of my league.

She was not alone in her office, but was deep in conversation with a younger girl (probably in her early twenties), with luxuriously silky, long blonde hair. She had her back to me when I first entered the room, bending slightly over the desk, extenuating her curves. I couldn't see the front view but the back view was very tasty, even when it was stretched inside a Police uniform. When I walked into the room, they both turned to face me, and my unspoken question was answered. The front was indeed as attractive as the rear. She had a pale, fresh complexion, with just a touch of freckles around the nose, the deepest petrol-blue eyes that I had ever seen and (I was sure it was just for my benefit) a beautiful wide smile.

I think I am definitely going to like it here.

"PC 3489. I'm Tim. I've just started today and I was told to ask for Harry. I brought this too, for the Evidence Room", placing the bag of suspicious shredded plant material on the desk.

"That'll be me. I'm Harry, and this is Jenny, our Victim Support Officer," the darker one answered. "Grab yourself a coffee and take a seat," she invited, waving her hand across in the direction of a half full filter machine, sitting on top of the rather solitary, battered looking filing cabinet. "There should be a spare cup in the top drawer underneath. We won't be a moment and we'll show you around."

My luck's in - both of them.

As I helped myself to a welcome steaming cupful, I couldn't help but smile at the ridiculously surreal idea of expensive filter coffee in a gaudy mug, emblazoned with the logo "Sex maniac at work". No wonder that one was the "spare".

Is this some kind of hazing initiation?

I'd heard that workplaces like to wind up the new boy, but even when you're ready for it, you've just got to take it and say nothing or you'll never live it down.

If this coffee cup is all they are going to do, then I'm getting off lightly.

I sat down on a spare chair over in one corner, while I listened in on the remainder of their conversation. Half of it was right over my head, and I have to admit I hadn't got a clue what they were on about most of the time, but from the snippets of what they were saying, it seemed that a visit from the new Police Commissioner was expected any day and they were trying to find new storage facilities for some excess equipment. Some kinds of "restraints" from what I picked up. Jenny suggested storing some of it in the Evidence Room, and passing it off as "evidence".

I wonder what kind of stuff they are hiding if it can pass for evidence.

The main station (and some small outlying village lockups), were apparently under threat of closure due to Government reduced funding and Harry feared that attempts may be made to amalgamate it with County headquarters in the City. The visit from the Commissioner was thought to be also threatening to bring about a cleanup, axing "dead wood".

That did not sound good. I've only just got here.

Several times I thought that I caught Jenny making eye contact with me, but I tried to look the other way and pretend I wasn't looking (although every time, I could feel my face going hot, and I hoped that they didn't notice). I'm sure she was smiling too.

Perhaps she's playing a game with me.

Then Jenny said that she had to go - some kind of "appointment with the Reverend", and with that, she hurried off. As she was leaving I saw that she was smiling again, and I swear I saw her wink.

Was that aimed at me or at Harry?

That left me alone with Harry. She sat down in the rotating chair at her desk, turning it to face me, her legs crossed to reveal more than just an accidentally generous length of her shapely thighs.
"So, tell me about yourself then Tim?" she asked.
That was direct! I don't know what to say to that.
"I'm not sure quite what you want to know. I've recently finished at the Academy and this is my first placement".
"So do you come from around here?"
"No, not really. It just seemed a nice quiet town to start out at"

"So where were you living before? Did you have your own place?"
"No," I answered cagily.

"Ahh! Living with parents still..."

Now I feel a fool. She'll think I'm a Mummy's boy.

"So, did you have a girlfriend here in Westhaven? Is that why you chose us?"
I tried to fight against the tidal wave of heat racing up my face.

This is getting a bit third degree

"Nothing like that. I just felt it was time for a change"

I could see that she was enjoying this. She was getting off on making me squirm.

"Do you prefer brunettes, red heads or blondes", she smiled. "You seemed quite taken with our little Jenny. Perhaps we will have to do something about that."

"I think I will just keep you around the station for a few days, rather than send you out on the beat just yet. Call it a workplace induction. I could do with a bit of help on a few things."

Then she rose, straightening her dress, and walked towards me.

"Stand up and take off your jacket", she commanded. I didn't dare not to oblige, so unbuttoned my jacket, placing it across the seat and standing in front of her. Suddenly her hands were feeling my arms, her fingers trailing across my chest.
"My you're quite a bigger boy than I would have thought. You feel quite strong," she purred.
Then snapping away, "You might be useful, after all"

"So you like our little town? You say you think it is "nice and quiet"? It is charming in a quaint little way, but all is never quite as it seems you know. You'll be surprised when you get to know it. We like it though. It suits us, just as it is, so we would really prefer it if the Commissioner's visit goes quietly, and if he doesn't have too many changes planned."

"We don't have a lot of crime around here, and what trouble there is, we have our own little ways of dealing with it, so not everything ends up in the great paper trail. Unfortunately, that does mean that we are victims of our own success. The City boys look at our stats and think that we aren't needed, so would just love to transfer our services elsewhere. Some of the locals aren't happy, so we've got a bit of a "Keep it local" campaign being drummed up by some of them. So every now and again you might find us besieged by the reporter from the local rag and his bunch of loony Temperance flag wavers too."

"What did you think of our little station when you arrived?"

I hardly know what to say to that one. It looks a bit of a shit heap to be honest but I can't tell her that.

Looking down at my feet, shuffling them, in the hope that the floor would open for me, I lied blatantly, "It's a very nice building."

"No, it's a dump! But it's our dump and we'd like to keep it. The cuts have bitten into our maintenance budget now for a good few years, and there's little hope of it getting any better. Last year was about as bad as it got, with the water freezing in the pipes, and everyone sitting here in thermals. Something had to be done. So we have initiated a little "Private Enterprise" of our own. Toasty in here now isn't it? And we're gradually refurbishing the building too, one bit at a time. It's slow going, but we're getting there."

"Are you shocked?"

"So here it is then. You have a choice. You can head back down to the main office. Some of the others down there aren't exactly with us, but they've got big enough blinkers on that they don't notice anything. If you like, you can keep your head down while we look for a more suitable station for you, or you can join us. It won't exactly be text book academy though. Do you think you are up to it?"

I've only just got here and it looks like I might be out before lunch time. I've never been one for sudden hasty decisions before, but maybe it's time for things to change. I've had a lifetime of living at home in the Vicarage with my parents: tired of being a good little boy, not shaking the boat, not upsetting mother, never having a life. If it all goes tits-up, at least I'll have experienced something.

"Ok, I'm in" *Is that really me saying that? Shit! Now I've really done it.*

"Right. So pick up that bag of pot and follow me. We'll go for a little tour. I'll show you my domain and introduce you to my team."

At that, she led me off out of her room and down a dark side passageway, to a small but very solid looking door, reinforced with sheet steel, and fitted with substantial looking locks. I think it might have been a bit of a giveaway as to its purpose, but the sign on the door said "Evidence Room".

"Looks impressive, doesn't it? Would you be as impressed if I told you we lost the keys at the Christmas party three years ago and haven't been able to lock it since? It doesn't matter though. Nobody is going to steal it in here" she laughed.

She opened the door and pulled a cord, triggering the insane flickering of a fluorescent strip light on the blink and ready to pop anytime, revealing a small room, with heavy-duty solid wooden shelving all around the other three walls. The only other light came from a small, heavily grilled window, high up on the facing exterior wall, too small for even the smallest child to crawl through, even without the grill. The shelves were filled with all sorts of strange objects, with larger objects stacked on the floor around – positively an Aladdin's Cave. Hanging from hooks off some of the higher shelves on the far wall, were a selection of what could only be described as Fancy Dress outfits: furry animal onesies, French maid's costume, Captain Sparrow pirate, just to name a few.

She tossed the bag of cannabis into a square green plastic tub, just inside the door, and as it landed I was surprised to see that the tub was already almost full.

"Nearly ready for emptying" she said. "They get collected once a week, usually on a Thursday, and taken across to the Women's Institute. The ladies then share it out and spend the weekend baking. Then "Granny's Herbal Cakes" get distributed around by their helpers every Monday to their customers – mostly church halls, community centres, youth groups. We noticed years ago that when the neighbourhood youths are stoned out of their minds, they are too sleepy to misbehave. It was too haphazard to regulate though, so now we organise them through the youth groups, delivering a safer product with consistent dosage. It gives the old dears something to do with themselves, and it's bridging the age gap too. The youngsters are only too happy to help them. The cakes are delicious too. You really must try some.

She closed the door on the "Aladdin's Cave" and we set off once more back towards the main corridor, heading back towards the custody suite, stopping at another door signed "Blue Rest Room".

"You've seen part of how we keep the crime rate down around here. Are you ready now for our other little "Private Enterprise? All the same, even if you aren't really. You're in it up to your neck now," and she pushed the door open leading us into a comfortable common room, laid out with armchairs arranges around a central coffee table. On a larger table in the corner stood a top of the range version of one of those fancy machines for making all of those expensive coffees (as promoted on TV by that rather effeminate actor).

It wasn't the contrast of the luxurious decoration and furnishings of this room, as compared to the starkness of the rest of the station however, that really caught my eye but the occupants. Seated on a long settee smiling broadly at me, sipping on tall foaming lattés was a pair of absolute visions.

"You already know Lady Sabrina, otherwise known as Jenny" Harry introduced, waving her hand at the small, petite blonde, with the deep petrol blue eyes, whom I had already met. "She is our Police victim support officer and part-time Submissive S & M specialist." She giggled as she heard her introduction, this time blatantly offering me her widest, most welcoming smile. She was however, no longer wearing her regulation Police uniform. In its place she was wearing a glossy black, patent leather-effect playsuit, laced up the front with criss-crossing leather thongs, barely managing to restrain her very ample and obvious assets. On her wrists she wore black leather, studded cuffs and at her neck a pyramid-studded black leather dog collar. On her feet she wore long, patent thigh length boots with 6in needle sharp silvered heels.

Waving her hand again in the direction of the other vision of loveliness, she continued "and this is Lady Helena, known elsewhere by her other name of Angela. She is our Traffic warden and part-time Dominant S & M specialist." The "vision" smiled and winked at me in answer. She seemed a little older than Lady Sabrina, perhaps aged about 25yrs, with long, glossy jet black hair, blue eyes, and very pale, porcelain complexion (what I would probably describe as "Goth" style make-up), with luscious dark black/blood-red lips. Although seated, she seemed to be tall and slim, dressed as a Dominatrix: in a bright red latex, figure-hugging playsuit with multiple zips, her breasts divided by studded leather straps in matching red leather, which crossed her chest. On her feet she also wore long, patent thigh length boots with similarly needle-pointed silvered stiletto heels.

"So now you have met both of my "Ladies," Harry continued, "and from now on, you will use these preferred names in the workplace. Similarly, you should refer to me by my correct title of "Madame Sapphire". Together we operate our little "Private Enterprise" under our business name of "Blue". Although our existence is well known around the town, our location of operation remains secret. That is to say rather, it's "secret" only to Head Office in the City, the newspapers and the local Temperance league. Obviously we are very well-known to our many customers, and these include several magistrates, a vicar, a judge, and many other local pillars of the community."

Lady Helena broke in, with a deep and sultry purr, "In fact I have one of my gentlemen due for his regular "therapy" session. If you will excuse me, "Spanker" will be here at any moment," and rising from the sofa she glided effortlessly in her ferocious looking footwear out of the room towards her "dungeon".

Harry, or "Madame Sapphire" as I now must get used to calling her, laughed. "Wait until you meet our Spanker. He's a real character. He's also a prime example of the need for our services here. He has been unhappily married for years to a rather dowdy lady who likes to put all of her passion into her "good deeds", so he comes here for a bit of human contact. It's also where he can relax from his high-profile position as a town councillor, where he has to force himself into a persona that for him is un-naturally "dominant". In contrast, here he can relax into a "submissive" role, where Lady Helena makes his decisions for him. It is the only thing sometimes that protects his sanity.

That's the magic of what we do here. We provide the ultimate fantasy. If a guest feel downtrodden in their everyday life, they can come here and release their pent-up frustration in a safe, controlled environment, while re-enacting their ideal persona of being the dominant alpha-male. In contrast, someone who is in a high-pressure position, where they have to present to the world a hard and dominant façade that is against their true nature, can relax out of character for a short time. It may remind them of that time as a child when their mother ruled the household, or where a dominant school teacher made their decisions for them. They find it frees their soul from its invisible chains, if only for just a short time."

She then went on to explain how the cells were now used more for business than for miscreants, in fact these being the first parts of the building to have been renovated, ploughing back some of the profits, as an obvious business investment. That is why there are no spare cells at present. Cells are not really needed, so only the bare minimum of a couple are retained, as there is very little crime in the town. Trade from "Blue" is roaring, with their "personal services" keeping customers too exhausted for any other activities; and the confectionary sideline ensures that any other potential troublemakers are maintained in too docile a state for them to misbehave.

She was however worried about the possible danger of closure: along with the loss of earnings which have been supplementing the Station's budget, would be the loss of the valuable facility to the town which has been helping to retain its quiet and peaceful quaintness. She was concerned that they may have to relocate to other premises. A Police Station was so much safer an environment to work from, than any other location could possibly offer.

"For the time being", she continued, "I think we will make use of you in a security capacity, and in that way you can watch how we operate and learn the business. At the same time, you will be available to help out by lending us a bit of muscle power now and again, for a bit of lifting and carrying."

With that she led him into another room off the main corridor, marked "CCTV control room", where a wall of screens displayed the images being recorded on cameras set in every room in the station. In front of these was a central console with a series of buttons and dials, and a high-backed, rotational controller's chair in the middle.

Bidden to take my place in the deeply padded control seat, upholstered in soft, black leather, the sensual aromas of leather, mixed with citrusy, orange oil leather polish tempted my senses. Madame Sapphire leaned seductively across my body (deliberately, but not I must say, without my appreciation), while she instructed me on how to view the current and retained recordings; make back-ups of images; change the cameras to toggle between different rooms; and to control the positioning of the cameras, zooming in and changing the angle on the action if required. Flicking through the different cameras I could see the counter area (where the counter clerk was dealing with customers); the interview rooms (currently unoccupied); and each of cells: one with its overnight drunk, currently still sleeping it off.

More importantly I could look into the refurbished cells, which had now been converted into "dungeons" tailored specifically to the tastes of each of the three ladies: these were the Blue room (Sapphire's dungeon); the Red Room (Lady Sabrina's dungeon); and the Black Room (Lady Helena's dungeon). The rooms all followed a similar theme, with a bed, a chest of drawers and wall racks holding an array of weapons, including canes and whips, but also each contained a few extra items, apparently these being specific to each of their "Specialities".

Comfortably installed in my new position of CCTV Controller, I was experimenting with the various buttons, practising zooming and rotating the cameras, feeling quite full of my new self-importance, and pondering on my good luck, when Lady Sapphire broke the moment by giving me a full box of tissues, saying she would collect me later – and with that, she left.

* * *

3 A REGULAR GUEST

From the vantage point of my CCTV camera, Lady Helena's Black Room looked both luxurious and terrifying at the same time. Despite the camera providing colour images, the scene was almost monochrome, with a polished black marble floor and black, soft "suede effect" flocking on the walls, contrasting against the polished chrome and steel of some of the equipment hanging from the walls and ceiling.

In common with the other two dungeons, the Black room contained the basic furniture of a chest of drawers (presumably to hold some of her smaller pieces of equipment) and a large, ornately carved "antique-style" bed (in this room being fitted with beautiful white satin sheets). On one wall there was also a purpose-built rack carrying a selection of canes, whips and other fiendish looking weapons (including paddles, flails, ticklers, soft suede flogger and a long "cat of nine tails").

In addition, the room contained those items which appealed more specifically to Lady Helena: a leather-covered padded bench placed at the end of the bed, and a large wooden wheel standing against one wall which had been fitted with a series of four cuffs around the rim, which probably served as restraints for wrists and ankles. Finally, at the end of the room was an impressive looking high-backed chair – No, I think it would be better described as being more like a throne.

As I looked across nervously at the screen, I saw the door into the Black room open. Lady Helena was the first to enter the room, strutting on her ridiculously high, needle-heeled boots, every inch of her screaming "Dominatrix", dressed in her red latex, figure hugging playsuit. Behind her, a middle-aged man followed, his eyes firmly fixed on the floor, never daring to look up at her. He was tall and thin, with slightly stooped, rounded shoulders. He had white/grey hair receding in the middle, a long, thin face with narrow lips, wearing horn rimmed glasses over tired-looking eyes, swollen with very noticeable dark, heavy bags. I had no idea who he was, but no doubt I would find out soon enough. This must have been "Spanker", the "Regular customer" whom Lady Helena had been expecting for his "therapy" session.

It felt very wrong to sit there and watch them, but at the same time it was fascinating and irresistible. They had no idea that I was watching, but I was sure that Lady Helena at least would have been only too pleased to think that I could see her. In fact I think she would have really been turned on by it. Lady Sapphire too. She had positively "forced" me to sit and watch.

They want you to watch. Don't be a wuss! Just enjoy the view.

Besides, I was fascinated to find out what all of those things were for. There was no way that I was going to let any of those girls know that I hadn't even broke my duck yet. Better keep quiet on that one or they might show me the door. If I'm lucky I might get some action.

Thought you were saving yourself?

That is what my mother had always made a big thing about – this waiting for the right girl; that sex was only for married people to keep up the family name. What the hell does a family name matter anyway? Especially one like "Titterington".

That's what I've been telling you for years. You took your time to listen didn't you?

You'd better just sit there and enjoy it. You aren't going anywhere for a while just yet. Your trouser area isn't behaving itself enough to be seen in mixed company. You'll probably be needing those tissues soon.

As I watched, my eyes magnetised to the screen, Lady Helena strutted up and down in front of her "victim". As she passed the wall rack, she reached up and picked out a short whip, testing it against her open palm as she walked.

How on earth do you work the sound on this machine? I'm going to have to guess what is happening, like some kind of perverted mime show.

She raised her other arm and pointed towards Spanker, her finger outstretched. Clearly she was ordering him to do something. He nodded his head and started to remove his clothing. Obviously it was not fast enough for her liking, as I could see her now shouting at him, and he fumbled with the buttons of his shirt, almost tearing it in his haste trying to remove it more quickly. Soon he was cowering before her, stark naked save for his hands folded across his package, trying to retain his modesty.

Then the whip cracked out, licking off the backs of his hands, making him flinch, tucking them away behind him. The whip cracked once more, the tip dancing across his privates, and his hands shot back to the front again. She was now standing there laughing at him, her head back, her long, jet black hair, tossed back over her head.

She barked another command and he scurried to the leather covered bench, where he picked up some small leather objects. I couldn't quite figure what they were at first, but then he started to climb into them. It was an item of black leather clothing.

Oh, noooo! - a thonged posing pouch!

The sight of his puny, saggy middle-aged body in black leather budgie smugglers was just not right, and I almost wet myself trying not to laugh. Then she threw him something and barked out another command. He fastened the object around his neck (a leather studded dog collar, with the word "Submissive" picked out in studs), then knelt on the floor at her feet. Strutting around him until she stood behind him, trailing the tip of her whip across his head as she went, she grasped what little hair he had still on his head, pulling it back towards her, and tied a blindfold around his eyes.

While she busied herself blindfolding her victim, depriving him of his visual senses, I took the opportunity to glance away at the console, from one control to another until I found the settings for sound, I turned the dial, exactly at the same instant that she cracked her whip, licking the sharp tip across his manhood. The "crack" of the whip and his "yelp" of pain took me by surprise and made me jump in my seat.

She again ordered him to stand and raise his hands, "encouraging" his every move with well directed licks of her whip, then drawing down a polished steel bar from the ceiling, which must have been on some form of pulley system, she shackled his wrists into restraints at each end. She then pulled on the pulley rope, taking up the tension and stretching his arms just enough that his heels were barely touching the floor. I could see his chest rising and falling rapidly, and his teeth tightly clenched together, as the shame and discomfort excited his body. His excitement was also borne out by the signs of his awakening erection stirring inside that ridiculous thong, which became more and more evident as she now teased at his raised and protruding nipples with every tortuous crack of her whip.

Now she stroked at his chest, down the trail towards his navel, first with her whip and then with the tips of her perfectly manicured blood-red nails. She bowed her head towards him and I could see her as she blew gently on his nipples, then licked and swirled her tongue around and around, once more then following that trail down toward his lower extremities. Reaching his thong, the tip of his manhood could be seen over its edge, trying frantically to escape its leather restraints. Then taking the flesh of his foreskin in her teeth, she teased and stretched him, taking little nips from time to time, his breath visibly taking little gasps with each nip.

As I watched him holding his breath, and gasping with pain with each sharp yet blissful nip, I realised that I too was echoing his every movement, my uncontrollable erection also battling to escape the confines of my pants. As she stroked at his trail and back across his stomach, she flicked the ties on his thong, allowing his shaft to spring free, standing proud and expectant, glistening with the moisture of anticipation. He visibly groaned in pleasure at its release, his eyes closed, teeth firmly clenched, momentarily holding his breath as he exhaled. I too followed his every agony, and, unable to stand one more second, was forced to free my own ecstatically swollen member.

Her fingers continued stroking his body, stroking him along his shaft and massaging his scrotum, grasping its girth and pumping it relentlessly up and down. I also, in the privacy of my control room, imagined the pleasure of her touch, echoing her actions on my own grateful member.

I watched as her fingers explored further, probing his anus deeply, massaging in a circular motion, causing his body to buck and making him cry out. Then she pulled out, ordering him to suck her fingers, wiping the moisture once more down his central trail. Reaching across to the bench she then picked up a curious object - flesh coloured and similar in shape to a man's penis.

A dildo? No! She just turned it on. It is electrical. It's some kind of vibrator.

Now she replaced her finger with the vibrator, forcing it deeper and deeper inside him. I could see his stiffened erection as she once more grasped it firmly, greedily licking its length, then massaging it up and down. At first she teased it slowly; then building speed; then slowing down once more. Repeatedly and relentlessly she teased him; speeding up again; now teasing at the end with the tip of her tongue; before taking his full length deep into her mouth.

How deep is she going to take that in? That girl could swallow a cucumber whole!

Suddenly she pulled away, the moisture of her lips trailing from her prey. Then deftly tearing at a small package, she grasped his shaft firmly in one hand, unrolling the condom skilfully down its length. Without hardly any loss of momentum, once more she continued pumping and driving her hands up and down his length, relentlessly building speed; massaging him behind his scrotum with a small vibrating device. I also continued to pump away on "the best toy in town", reaching across to that now welcome box of tissues and grasping a fistful. Spanker was now straining with all of his strength against his restraints, twisting to the left and to the right as he writhed in a mixture of combined pain and ecstasy, his eyes closed, his teeth biting down on his lower lip. His breathing was now coming in gasps, panting; rivers of perspiration running down his cheeks. Finally his entire body appeared to convulse and shake, as he exploded into the condom, while at the same time I did the same.

Thank God for those tissues.

As Spanker just hung there, his body drained, his energy completely spent, Lady Helena reached up and unshackled him, allowing him to slide limply to the floor. Stepping over his prone body without even a second glance, she snapped at him "Clean yourself up!", and, as an afterthought added "and then the room....and make sure you do a good job or you'll be punished some more".

She then turned and gave him a sharp, hard thrash across the buttocks with her crop, before stalking off out of the door.

"Yes Mistress. Thank you mistress," Spanker called after her adoringly.

* * *

4 A NATURAL LOSS

Over the next few days, I found myself dividing my time between regular Police duties and working for "Blue", although I would have preferred to have been exclusively occupied with the latter. However, Sergeant Toscer had other ideas and insisted on taking me out on patrol with him a couple of times, to "show me the town".

Even on the second day, I had been heading down the central corridor towards the Common Room when he had caught me, ushering me out to the patrol car. Although I was interested in getting to know the various hotspots of the town (the licensed premises, the betting offices, the parks where youths tended to congregate at night), the prospect of even a half day stuck in the car with him didn't endear me. Sitting in the patrol car with him that morning just confirmed my reticence. It was like sitting in a dustbin.

Although he was no longer permitted to smoke in the vehicle, it was obvious that Tosser was in fact a chain smoker, evidenced by more ash than could be found on top of Pompeii – and not just in the "ashtrays" but in every other part of the dashboard and steering column niches, and a thick layer sitting in the creases of the gear stick cover. Added to that, the floor in the passenger foot well, at the front and in the back, was covered in the wrappings of many discarded MacDonald's meals, interspersed with tightly screwed up bundles of white paper (the remains of countless trips to the "fish and chip" shop). Empty cans of Coke were also scattered around on the floor, lying abandoned on their sides (the sticky contents having long ago trickled out and seeped into the carpet), along with their cardboard counterparts, residual from late-night drive-in takeaways. Even more disturbing were the screw-top plastic cola bottles, half filled with a yellowy liquid bearing no resemblance to the original contents. *The dirty b@****d!*

As soon as we set off, it was apparent that he had an ulterior motive to just patrolling the street. He just wanted to get me alone to ask if had found any dirt on Harry yet (dirt that I suspected would have been used as ammunition to prise his way into one or all of the girl's beds). I shook my head and told him "no, not yet".

Paying more attention to his over-vivid imagination than to the road around him (narrowly missing first the rear end of a bus, then an elderly lady attempting to cross at a zebra crossing), he took great delight in regaling me with his boastful accounts of what he "would like to do to that Victim Support girl" (obviously Sabrina), and "the other one", "the traffic girl" (Helena), and how he was going to get what he wants.

It was my disgust at his conversational skills, even more than his driving abilities and the condition of his vehicle that really made my stomach clench up. I could feel the early stages of salivation that usually pre-empted an early re-emergence of my last meal. It then filled me with great relief when I realised that we were stopping, as he pulled the car up into the car park of one of the town centre pubs. I couldn't wait to escape into the fresh air, if only for even a short respite.

The Cross Keys Hotel, like most of the rest of the town, reflected the glories of Victorian splendour, now long since past. It would have once been an expensive hotel, catering to the holiday needs of the wealthier slice of society, as they whiled away their summers taking in the healthy seaside air. Now those days were long gone. It had many years ago ceased to function as a hotel, save for a short-lasting venture (in the years prior to the opening of "Blue", which had since cleaned up the sleazier aspects of town life), when some of the rooms had been rentable "by the half hour" for non-sleeping purposes. Now most of the upper floors were uninhabitable, most of the windows broken (although one or two did have residual traces of scraps of rags stuffed into the smaller holes), and the only living residents that these rooms ever saw these days had feathers. The town centre pigeons had taken over.

Reaching into the back of the car to grasp a chipped and battered baseball bat, which he tucked into the back of his belt, Tosser bade me "Keep it shut, lad. Just follow my lead and for God's sake try to look a bit hard!" With that he set off up the few stone steps of the main entrance, two at a time, kicking the heavy wooden doors open to add dramatic effect. To my shame, I followed him in.

At the sight of us the few shabbily dressed customers in the bar furtively slid out through the door behind us, not wanting to be involved in any trouble. Crossing to the bar, Tosser was like a crazy man possessed, his face red, his eyes flashing with rage. Reaching behind his back he drew out the bat and with one long sweep, cleared the counter for its full length of every glass, full or empty. Stamping through the sea of beer and broken glass underfoot, he pushed his way behind the bar, grasping the manager by the throat. "I've come for my money, and no more excuses from you this time!"

Throwing the manager aside like a child's toy (no mean feat, as this man was not small, looking more like a human-gorilla cross breed), he then brought his bat down hard on the side of the till, the drawer bursting open in surrender.
"That'll do for a start!"

Snatching a bundle of notes, which he stuffed in his trouser pocket, he then turned his attention to a small door at the far end of the bar area, kicking that open to gain access to the small rear office. Following him through behind the counter, I watched dumbfounded as he pressed a series of buttons on the CCTV control box, setting it into reformat mode. He was erasing the entire memory!

Then he re-emerged, jabbed the manager sharply in the stomach with the bat handle and threatened to prosecute him for not having his CCTV turned on. "I'll be back for the rest tomorrow!"

Not with me you won't

I followed him back to the car like an automaton. I had never seen anything like it. I thought we were supposed to be the good guys. A torrent of conflicting emotions washed over me. Shock and disgust at what I had just witnessed, and deep, deep shame to have stood there and done nothing to prevent it. But how could I expose him though, another policeman? Apart from the publicity that would have been bad for the station, more importantly nobody would believe me. He was a long-standing and experienced officer and I was just a rookie. A new boy! I would then be a pariah for whistle-blowing. I would never be able to work in the Police again.
I will have to keep quiet.

The thought of doing nothing though was just as bad. As I had felt ashamed to watch and do nothing, now I felt even more ashamed to go along with it and help him to keep his secret. Also, by going along with it, I was placing myself right where he wanted me – under his control for the rest of my time here. He would be able to threaten me with colluding and assisting him, just for saying nothing. I was now as guilty as he was – his accomplice.
Damn him!

On way back to the station, as we were driving past the town botanical park, I saw a small figure pedalling away furiously on his bicycle and recognised him immediately. It was Luke Thompson, the boy from yesterday who had been arrested by Tosser "in possession". He was presumably now out on his bike delivering those cakes for the Women's Institute (a form of "Community Service" suggested to him as an alternative to a Police record). I was just contemplating how the boy had had himself a lucky escape yesterday, when all of a sudden I felt the car lurch to the left.
WTF!!!

Tosser had deliberately swerved across the road to knock him off, screeching to a halt in front of the pile of twisted metal and small boy now lying in the gutter. Jumping from the passenger side, I ran to try to help him, untangling his legs from the frame and extracting his left foot from between the bent spokes of his front wheel. From behind me I heard the footsteps of the Sergeant, and in the corner of my eye saw him pick up the bike and throw it over the brick wall of the park. Pushing past me, Tosser then picked up the injured boy by the scruff of his neck. Thinking that I was distracted by the hand clutching Luke's collar, with his other hand he furtively stuffed a small package into the boy's pocket (*He just planted more pot on him!!*). Then making a big show for my benefit of pretending to find it, he arrested him once more "for possession".

This is now beyond disgusting! I have to do something..I have to think of a way...but how?

On the drive back to the station, with Luke cowering on the back seat, afraid to move from where he had been thrown, Tosser continued boasting of his plans for the girls.

Parking up in the bays in the alleyway behind, he paused for a couple of minutes to rough the boy about a bit more, then took him inside again, handing him to the Custody Officer as before, along with the new bag of "suspicious organic material" (pot), directing him to "not be soft" and to "throw the book at him this time". I followed along behind, hands thrust deep in my pockets, scuffing my shoes along on the floor as I slouched along, wanting desperately for no-one to see me with him and to disassociate myself from the whole rotten deal.

However, as we left the Custody Suite, on our way back to the General Office, somebody did see us. Approaching us down the narrow corridor, with no possible passing place to duck into was Sabrina. An evil leer broke out across his face. Tosser had seen Sabrina and she had no escape.

He leaned across the narrow passageway, with his hand above his head, flat against the opposite wall, so that she was obliged to duck and wiggle sideways underneath. Stepping forward at that last second, he crushed her back against the wall with his chest, leering down the front buttons of her blouse and breathing down her neck as he whispered into her ear. "How about it tonight then my little poppet? I can book us a night of unbridled passion at the Grand Empire Hotel, down on the Prom. I'll give you such a good seeing to it'll make your teeth rattle!"

Uuurghh!! He makes my skin crawl just to hear him. How can she put up with that without puking?

I could feel the heat of anger rising up at the back of my neck, as I gripped my fists tightly at my side, fighting against myself not to tear him apart, limb from limb.

No! that isn't the way. I've got to think up something though to see to him!

As she wriggled free from him, and scurried off down the corridor to the relative safety of the other girls and the Common Room, like a tiny mouse desperately breaking free from the clutches of a cobra, Tosser sighed to himself triumphantly.
"See how she can hardly keep her hands off me!" Then he turned back towards the outside door, to go back out on patrol. "coming?"

But there was no way that I was going to be going out with him again in that car any time soon. So, I made an excuse that I had some urgent work to do in the Evidence Lock up, and he grunted and left to go back out without me.

Thank God for that!

Heading back down to the Custody Suite, the officer of the day was only too pleased to see me, particularly when I pulled the arrest sheet and told him to release the boy. Sliding the arrest sheet into the shedding machine, I took great satisfaction in listening to the grinding, tearing noise as it ate the sheet of paper, destroying all evidence of the boy's arrest. Then, leading Luke back out through the rear door of the Station into the alleyway behind, I told the boy to get off home and to avoid the area for a few days.

I headed back to the Common Room for a welcome and warming

cup of latté, relieved at having got out of having to spend another second in that car with Tosser, when I saw the two girls, Sabrina and Helena, curled up together on the sofa, consoling each other. Both were upset about Tosser. He had apparently been threatening both of them, but Sabrina especially had been being pushed to meet him for his promised "night of passion" where he was "going to teach her a few things". He had told her how he thought she was pure and untouched and he wanted to be the man to "corrupt her".

I felt helpless. My feelings of shame and impotence from earlier, when I had failed to act on the intimidation of the publican and the brutalisation of the young boy, came back to haunt me as I tried to reassure her. I tried to get her to be strong (even though I secretly knew that I had not been so when it had been my turn), and told her not to go. I promised that I would think of something to sort him out (and this time I meant it!).

But first I had a few things to do, while I planned out my course of action, so telling Sapphire that I was just taking some more equipment to the village lock up, I headed off out once more. On the way I met up with another of the more regular customers just leaving after a session with Madame Sapphire, recognising him as Chair of the Young Farmer's Association, Hugh Johnson. We chatted for a few minutes as we walk out towards the rear car park. An idea had begun to form in my head....

Driving across to the lock up in the Dog Handler's van with yet another stash of furry animal outfits from the Evidence Lock up bundled up in the back, I paused on the way to collected the bike from the park bushes, then stashed the lot in the small windowless brick building on the edge of the nearby village, just outside of town. It would all be safe in there until after the Commissioner's visit.

At every opportunity after that, as soon as I got to the Station I would find myself some excuse to slope off and join the girls in their Common Room, where I busied myself in getting friendly with the Ladies, in particular with Lady Sabrina, and making sure that Tosser hadn't been bothering them again. As she had suggested, Madame Sapphire had plenty of jobs for me to do: helping her to move her more specialised "equipment" from where it had been kept (in both the Weapons Room and the Evidence Room), taking it to temporary storage in several of the outlying village "lock-ups"; and acting as her private "Security Officer", watching over things in the CCTV control room.

Yesterday was a little strange however (my sixth day at the Station), when I had come back into the Common Room after a morning of moving yet more of Madame Sabrina's "special" equipment. It had been a hot and dusty job. My mouth felt like the bottom of a bird cage and I was spitting feathers for a long, cold drink (literally spitting feathers, as there had been some particularly loose and fluffy feather boas in one of the boxes that had really given me an explosive sneezing fit measurable I am sure as at least a level 6 on the Richter scale). My uniform too was covered in dust and feathers, looking as though I had been wrestling with "Big Bird" off "Sesame Street" – or at least "Big Bird" after a fluorescent pink dye job! It had to be done. As I was now safely out of the public view, I took off my jacket to give it a shake and pick off the worst of the feathers, tossing it down on the armchair behind me. I could still feel those damned itchy feathers though. Some must have gone down inside the neck of my shirt and were tickling my back. So loosening my tie, then sliding it off, to join my discarded jacket, I unbuttoned my shirt. It was only then, as I pulled my shirt back off my shoulders, my eyes cast downwards looking for feathers, that I felt six eyes burning like knives into my flesh. I looked up and realised I was not alone. Not only that, but I was actually the floorshow.

I did begin to wonder a little if perhaps the reason for moving all of this equipment was not entirely to do with a general tidy-up for the Police Commissioner's visit, but maybe had the ulterior motive of providing the ladies with the "entertainment" of making me perform some manual labour while they sat and watched.

Everything generally was going great though. There was just one problem. When the girls were all together it was not so bad (in fact it was good fun), but whenever I was alone with Lady Sabrina it was embarrassing. I just kept getting tongue-tied and couldn't manage to say any of the things I meant to say. What was it about that girl that turned me into such a basket case.

It wasn't just vocal too. I suddenly developed two left feet and sausage fingers, tripping over everything, even when there was nothing there to trip on, and dropping almost everything I tried to pick up. It wasn't that she intimidated me in her Dominatrix persona (although I must admit that she did kind of freak me out a bit when she had all of the gear on), because she usually kept most of it covered up in a silk wrap. Actually, that was worse. It left more to the imagination and drove me wild.

I know it's crazy, when you think how I had watched her performing with her "guests", but I just wanted to ask her out for a drink, wearing ordinary clothes. I just struggled to put it into words though and kept on changing the subject.
I'm sure she must think I am some kind of idiot.

That's because you are an idiot.

Then, after about a week of dallying around the subject, I finally plucked up the courage and asked her out. To my immense surprise she had said yes. Suddenly I could talk to her normally without eating my teeth and could walk in a straight line without falling over my big feet. Then we realised the real problem. When could we actually go out? We were always in the Station working. So it was a date that wasn't a date, while we waited to find a time when we could sneak away. In the meantime would keep it our little secret.

It was a day much like all those before really, I was once more in the CCTV control room keeping an eye on things (only by now I had become almost an expert in operating the controls – one handed most of the time for obvious reasons): Spanker was in the Black room with Lady Helena for his daily "session"; and a regular customer, Bob Deadwood (generally known as "Old Bob"), had arrived for his "usual" with Lady Sabrina. I must admit I had felt more than just a few pangs of jealousy when I thought of Old Bob with Sabrina, but when I saw him I could only feel pity. He was the wrong side of 90, balding (save for straggly wisps of white hair around the edges), short and painfully thin, slightly stooping, and really not in good health. In fact he was barely able to shuffle along using his zimmer for support.

When I first switched the camera controls over, to bring up Sabrina's "Red Room", it was still empty. It was very much similar in appearance to the other two rooms ("Black" and "Blue" – how appropriate for BDSM dungeons, where the patrons may probably emerge "black and blue"). It also had a highly polished floor (classy but functional, for easy cleaning of blood or any other body fluids), and plain coloured, flocked "suede" effect walls, in this case being dark burgundy coloured. This apparently was just the outer surface finishing of substantial sound proofing, installed in each room to discretely disguise the presence of the patrons and their more "energetic" activities. Also, in common with the other rooms, there was the ubiquitous chest of drawers (no doubt similarly equipped with the smaller requisites essential to her "performance": assorted clamps, cuffs, plugs and vibrators), and wall rack display of larger pieces of punishment equipment (canes, paddles, flails, whips, ticklers, soft suede flogger and long "cat-of-nine-tails"). As in Lady Helena's room there was a tall, high backed chair against the wall at one end and one of those strange forged iron "wheel" devices, fitted with four cuff restraints, against the other wall. In the centre of the other wall stood an equally beautiful king-sized bed, this time elaborately carved in dark mahogany, and covered in this case by deep, blood-red satin sheets. At the foot of the bed, stood once more, a matching bench deeply padded with burgundy leather.

I could hear music playing softly: smooth and relaxing instrumental pieces, the attempt to create a relaxing ambience of the soft music and satin sheets, contrasting sharply with the disturbingly oppressive visual assault from the array of harsh steel and leather implements of torture around the room.

The heavy cell door creaked slowly open and the fragile, old man (balding with just a few traces of wispy white hair around the sides) shuffled in, parking his zimmer frame to one side of the door and kneeling with great difficulty beside it. However, I paid him little attention, my eyes transfixed by the vision of loveliness that strutted in behind him.

Lady Sabrina was no longer wearing her all-encompassing silk kimono, with which she usually disguised herself. She was now dressed in full Dominatrix mode (not in the slightest part depicting her other supposed role, described previously as "an occasional submissive" – this was beautiful, yet at the same time, terrifying): she wore black lace-edged high-legged lycra shorts, crossed by black chiffon straps, latticed tightly around her upper body, criss-crossing across her ample breasts, restraining yet supporting them, while revealing her nipples. Each nipple had been pierced, with a silver ring passing through. Two fine silver chains then passed from each nipple ring to the centre of a pyramid-studded black leather dog collar. She wore similar, but wider, black leather cuffs, also with pyramidal studding, around each wrist and each thigh, on the outer edge of each provided with a rotational D-ring. Affixed to the rings on her thigh cuffs trailed long, knotted black thongs, or jesses (possibly intended for potential restraint purposes, but which also served to flail the wearers legs as she stalked around the room).

In her hand she carried a short riding crop, absent-mindedly toying with its end as she stalked past the grovelling figure at her feet. Turning, with a gentle smile across her lovely features, she cracked the crop harshly across the paper thin skin on his back. He winced in agony, yet smiled up at her adoringly.

How I wished that was me kneeling at her feet...

"Don't look at me!" she commanded.

"No, Mistress" and he averted his eyes, his smile widening.

Then pointing with the crop, she ordered him to undress.

"Yes Mistress."

He unfastened his clothes with shaking hands (although I could not help feeling that they shook more from his advanced age rather than fear, because of the excited smile on his face), and placed them in a neat pile under his zimmer. It was then that I noticed that he was not wearing the usual "old man" Y-front underwear, but had been already dressed under his street clothes in a skimpy leather thong.

Standing in front of him, her legs slightly apart, she bent down towards him, her long legs straight, her full breasts heaving just in front of his eyes, as she clipped a leather dog collar and lead around his neck. His eyes bulged with pleasure at the vision in front of him, and I begrudged him every second of it.

The taking his lead in her hand, she crossed to the bed, with him crawling on all-fours behind her. Pointing to the blood-red satin sheets she bade him lie on the bed. Still on his hands and knees, he crawled up with shaking hands on to the bed and rolled over, facing up, panting with the exertion. Then like a well trained puppy, he compliantly raised his hands above his head, as he must have done many times before, while she restrained first his wrists and then his ankles in soft leather cuffs, chained to the legs of the bed..

Watching her at her work, I couldn't help thinking, despite the harshly commanding Dominatrix persona, just how gentle she was being with him. She had allowed him to crawl to the bed and crawl up on to it, as part of the pretence of the domination scenario, where in reality she was preserving the dignity of the poor old soul who could not have gotten there any other way. He seemed to have been enjoying every second of it too (as so would I have done, wishing to have been in his place). At his age, what else would he have been doing with his life? Probably sitting in an armchair in an old folk's home, surrounded by a bunch of snoring old fossils, just waiting for God. She was giving him a new lease of life. I'll bet he lasts an extra good few years because of it too.

As I continued to watch her own version of "Help the Aged", I saw her working on his aged and wrinkled body, stroking down his body with a feather teaser; starting at his neck, trailing across to his nipples and down his trail towards his stomach. His head was arched backwards, his eyes tightly closed, his lips curled up into the widest smile. Then I saw her reach across to the bench, replacing the teaser with something else. The crop!

She continued for just a few moments, lightly biting on his nipples with the crop; then replacing it she changed to just her hands: her fingers gently stroking him. Reaching out again, now she held a small bottle, pouring the oily liquid in a trail over his chest and down the trail towards his thong, massaging his body with those soft gentle hands and beautifully manicured blood red nails, until his entire torso was glistening and wet.

I watched in awe as her long talons, stroked down the centre of his chest towards his thong, like some kind of large and dangerous feral cat playing with her prey. Then her hands slowly moved towards the ties holding his pouch in place....

Enough! Stop! I can't watch any more of that!

I quickly flicked the switch, changing the camera to another room. Any room. That was just too much. I couldn't sit here and watch Sabrina, my Sabrina, doing that to an old man.

* * *

Toggling through the camera images I came to Lady Helena's Black Room. Helena was wearing her usual costume of red latex, figure hugging playsuit with multiple zips, and studded straps which crossed her chest, dividing her luscious breasts. On her feet she wore long, patent leather, thigh-length boots with 6 in needle-sharp silvered heels.

She was also not alone.

She was accompanied by her usual daily regular customer – apparently, so Madame Sapphire advised me, a distinguished member of our local council, Councillor Rupert Rogers, to be known inside "Blue" only by his alias of "Spanker", in order to preserve his anonymity (a vain hope really for someone who ordinarily positively courts the attentions of the "paparazzi" of the local newspaper). He had arrived for his daily "therapy" session with Lady Helena.

Spanker, was kneeling on the floor of the dungeon, just inside the entrance, naked apart from a studded leather thong covering his embarrassment, panting with excitement and anticipation at the thought of the humiliation ahead of him.

Lady Helena entered the room, crossed to the music player sitting on top of the chest of drawers and turned it on. Instantly the room filled with the sound of a familiar piece of classical music. Where had I heard that before? Then it came to me. Of course. How appropriate. It was Ravel's Bolero. So famous all of those years ago, used by those Olympic skaters, then cheekily referenced in the bedroom scenes of that comedy film "10".

Now she moved to the wall rack, and reached for a leather collar and lead hanging from it. She then returned to her quarry and fixed it firmly around his neck. Taking his lead in her hand, she returned to the chest, leading Spanker behind her, and opening the second drawer, containing an array of butt plugs. Taking each object out of the drawer at a time, fingering them lightly, toying with the contents: fingering them; stroking their length, feeling their girth. Finally she made her choice and choosing the largest size.

Pulling on Spanker's lead, drawing him in towards her, she placed the heavy metallic object in his mouth, ordering him to "Suck!" then, pulling him once more by the lead, she commanded him to "Crawl!" on all fours towards the leather covered bench. As he crawled along the floor, she licked lightly at his nipples and the more sensitive part of his balls with her riding crop. At the bench she bade him wait while she fitted a full-face, fitted leather "gimp" mask on him, with round openings for his eyes, nose and mouth (the former being firmly zipped shut), and a large zipped closure reaching from the top of the head, down the back to the nape.

Ordered to bend over the bench, Spanker felt blindly for the bench and immediately complied, receiving a sharp crack across his behind from the riding crop by way of encouragement:

"Yes, Mistress" came a muffled splutter from behind the large plug inserted in his mouth like a baby's dummy.

"Grasp the legs of the bench!"

I was then presented with the ridiculous view that would remain with me as grotesque mental imagery, no doubt for the rest of my life, of Spanker, bent over the low, padded bench, naked apart from the skimpy leather thong, his backside in the air, held aloft by his spindly little legs. Tugging on the ties securing the sides of his thong, Lady Helena released the sides, freeing his buttocks to the air.

Crack!!

She brought the riding crop down sharply across his naked buttocks at full force, leaving a bright red wheal as evidence of its contact. Then in contrast, as though applying salve to his injury, she squeezed some form of cream lubricant from a large tube onto his rear and began to massage it with soft caresses from her experienced hands. He sighed deeply and groaned with pain and pleasure combined. With his backside now glistening from the lubricating cream, she raised her hand to full height and brought it swiftly down again, giving his rear a resounding slap, leaving a glowing red hand print in its wake. With the application once more of further lubricant, she continued to massage, pressing her hands now deeper beyond his cheeks, until she was now also massaging between his legs and onto his scrotum. With each inch that she massaged deeper, his body stiffened, then relaxed, accompanied by groans and gasps of shock and pleasure as she touched on the more sensitive parts.

Blinded to the world by his mask, with only his sensations of touch and the rhythmical sound of the accompanying music, he was helpless to prevent her every invasion of his body. Then she parted his cheeks, applying the nozzle of the tube directly to his anus, and inserted her finger deftly, to massage the lubricant deeply inside him, rotating her finger and pressing against the walls of his insides. Reaching around the front to his mouth, she quickly pulled out the plug, removing it without warning, causing his teeth to clink together, then equally without warning she forced the large, metallic object deep inside him.

He gasped and cried out in pain, his chest heaving as he panted with arousal. I felt my own stomach clench, as I felt the pain of his violation with him.

"We'll have none of that noise!" she commanded and reached around to place a ball-like object in his mouth. The "ball" had two straps, one coming from each side, and she brought these around his head to the back, closing them together with a ratchet-type fastening. Strange gurgling sounds were now all that he could manage, as the gag bit into the sides of his mouth.

Then she reached for a flat-sided paddle and struck him repeatedly across the backside, causing him to splutter more against his gag with the blistering pain, trails of saliva trickling down and dripping off onto the polished surface of the floor, as the paddle cut deep into his flesh.

She's really giving it to him today.

Finally, her frustration appearing to be vented, she stopped, pulling the plug from his anus and tossing it casually aside. She took a deep breath herself, and I realised that she had been as turned on by inflicting the pain as he had been by receiving it. She wiped her hand across the perspiration on her brow, product of all of the effort expended on him. Then regaining her composure, she ordered him to turn and to sit on the end of the bench, where she removed his gag.

Kneeling between his legs, hanging down at the end of the bench, she placed her hand flat on his stomach, pressing him back down on the bench, at the same time tearing away the remains of his thong and casting it aside. His pulsating member then sprang free in anticipation of what was yet to come. She grasped his now expanding shaft and began to work it; up and down, relentlessly, in time to the ambient music playing in the background. He gritted his teeth and groaned once more with pleasure and imminent relief.

I too felt obliged to imitate the actions witnessed unfolding before me, and I also freed my Little General and started to work him in matching rhythm.

I heard the now familiar sound of the tearing of a condom wrapper, watching as she continued to work his shaft, grasping it firmly driving it up and down. Then she paused very briefly while she unrolled the condom down his length, before returning to her rhythmical massaging, teasingly slowing, then building speed once more. As she worked him with one hand, her other hand reached between his legs and massaged his balls. Then reaching across to the bed she appeared to hold something small and plastic in her hand. Flicking a switch with her finger tip, the object sprung to life, with an electrical vibrating sound.

I've heard of these - a G-spot vibrator!

Touching it around his shaft and balls, subjecting him to teasing pulses, she continued to work his length (on occasions leaning down and running the tip of her tongue along the rubber sheathing his length. I struggled to keep my eyes open as I mirrored her movements, working my own length, but I could see that he was lying with his head twisted back, his eyes closed, breathing deeply, his chest rising and falling in uncontrolled passion.

We were both now very close. I reached for yet another fistful of the now welcome pack of tissues and closed my eyes. I could hear the slap of her hands as she worked him and the panting sounds from him as he gasped with her every stimulation. Now building more and more. He groaned loudly (as I did also at the same time) and we both exploded as we both reached orgasm together.

Once more, just as the last time that I had watched Lady Helena with Spanker, I heard her as she ordered him to clean the room before leaving or he will be punished.

"Yes Mistress. Thank you mistress".

* * *

Wiping myself down with the tissues, I switched the CCTV controls back to Lady Sabrina in her Red Room to see how she was getting on with Old Bob. I felt sure that she must be finished by now, as the old dude couldn't have had that much go in him. However, as the Red Room came back into view, I could see that his session was in fact far from over.

Old Bob was lying on his back on the satin sheets of the bed. Sabrina had climbed astride him facing backwards; sitting high on his chest. Pushing herself backwards, positioning herself over his face she commanded him "Lick me, you dirty little boy!" gyrating her hips and grinding down onto his face.

I closed my eyes for a second to imagine myself lying there in that position.

I opened them again to see her stretch out along his length, her breasts rubbing against his stomach, her arms outstretched. Then she pulled herself back up halfway, trailing her hands up his legs. With her hands on his hips, she pushed herself up as she pulled open the ties on his thong. As I watched, I saw his ancient manhood stiffen and spring back to life (more life than the rest of him appeared to possess), forcing itself free from its leather captor. It stood there proud and swollen above a mat of curly white hair, as though it were a triumphal column rising out of a cloud of white early-morning fog. She groaned in awe and appreciation as she grasped his length firmly in her hands (*God, this girl is such an actress*), then started to massage its length with those soft, sensual fingers. In my mind I could feel them as though it was my body she caressed, and my hands reached to my own "old friend" to see if I could bring him back to life as successfully as this, considering his exertions of just a couple of minutes earlier.

As she worked him (pumping first slowly to tease, then building speed, before teasingly slow once more), she ground her hips rhythmically into his face, bidding him to "Lick harder....lick my clit", her eyes closed, her head arched back, her long, golden hair thrown back along her back. Once more, I imagined myself lying there, receiving her ministrations, as I worked my old soldier once more.

God, this hurts. It hasn't seen this much action since I was twelve and I found that magazine in the park toilets. But I didn't let that stop me...

She bent forward once more, licking the length of his shaft with the tip of her tongue, swirling it around at its tip until it glistened under the gentle lights of the dungeon. Then, parting her moist full lips, she slid her mouth down over his member, taking it in right to the back of her mouth. Her head bobbed up and down as she repeatedly rose up then dove down deeper and deeper on his length, sucking him relentlessly, her long, silky mane falling forward over her face like a golden curtain. At the same time, her hips undulated as she ground herself down onto his face where he licked at her greedily. I could see his wrinkled chest, with its folds of yellowy-transparent, paper-thin skin, heaving with the exertion, turning to short panting bursts as he reached his climax, with a salty explosion into her mouth.

She lifted herself up, allowing his now limp and spent member to flop back down between his legs, wiping a small trail of semen from the corner of her lips with the back of her hands, then must have realised that he was no longer licking her.

"Wake up, you lazy boy"... she purred, sliding forwards off his face and turning to smile gently down at him.

Then her smile turned to horror, as her eyes met his cold, dead stare, his face a pallid white with a tinge of blue around the lips, his mouth curled up into an insanely happy smile.

She gave out the longest, most ear shattering scream that I have ever heard (even on the most blood-curdling late-night scary movie, watched from beneath the security of a comforting duvet – but here there was no duvet!), and leapt off his prone, limp body in blind panic.

Racing down the short corridor to the Red Room (almost losing my open trousers on the way), I frantically pulled the zipper up on my fly (nipping slightly the skin on the end of my "friend" in its teeth, in my haste). As I entered the room, gone was the vibrant and confident Dominatrix that I had been lusting over seconds earlier. Before me, in a whimpering mess, curled into foetal position in the corner of the room was a very small girl, sobbing inconsolably.

"He's dead...he's dead....I've killed him!"

I sat on the floor in the corner of the room, my arms wrapped around her protectively, vainly trying in some way to console her, as her body shook uncontrollably in waves of despair and desolation. Although from the moment I had met her, my all-consuming desire had been to hold her in my arms, but never like this. Now she seemed to be so fragile, so delicate, that she felt almost as though she might shatter into a million pieces at the slightest touch. Everything around us seemed distant and unreal, as though happening in slow motion.

All my carnal thoughts were now dissipated, and any erotic thoughts of making love to the most beautiful woman that I had ever cast my eyes upon, had evaporated into a distant memory. All I wanted now to do was to wrap her in cotton wool and hide her away from this – to wave a magic wand and make it all go away. As I held her, I also started to feel myself becoming racked by overwhelming guilt of what I had been doing when it had happened: how I had watched her ministering to his final act of passion, consumed at the time by thoughts of jealousy that it was not me receiving her attentions.

The first to appear was Lady Sabrina, alerted by the terrible screams despite the supposed "sound-proofing" of the rooms, dressed for the first time in my experience in her full Dominatrix clothing, having only the time to hurriedly pull over a silk kimono, although in my shock I barely registered the sight before me. She could have been wearing a full, all-encompassing hazmat suit for me and I wouldn't have noticed anything any different. She ran to the bed, taking Old Bob's hand in hers, and bizarrely, this once strong woman was also in floods of tears, distraught at the sight that lay before her.

Closely behind her came the Reverend Goodfellow. I had not even realised that he was visiting us today (in my naivety, I failed to notice that he was still adjusting his collar as he entered). He approached the bed on the other side, first taking Old Bob's hand to feel for a pulse, then reached up to his face and gently closed his eyes. Taking a small leather-bound bible out of his inside jacket pocket he knelt down and started murmuring, presumably giving him last rites.

The image then before me, of poor Old Bob expired on a giant bed of red satin sheets, flanked by a fully dressed Dominatrix and a minister of the church, set in a dungeon filled with every imaginable form of torture equipment was so surreal, I had to bite my lip to fight from the urge to laugh hysterically and uncontrollably.

After what seemed like an eternity, Lady Sapphire seemed to regain some of her composure and quietly left the room, returning a few minutes later accompanied by Spanker (now dressed more appropriately in his normal everyday manner, in keeping with his profession as an undertaker). Behind him, still in the corridor, stood a very white-faced Lady Helena.

"What do you suggest we do with him, Rupert ?" Madame Sapphire asked him (I was quite take aback to hear her referring to him for once using his everyday street name), "His family would be devastated to hear of it happening here".

"Don't worry. I'll take care of everything. It's what I do, remember?" he replied, patting the back of her hand comfortingly (it was almost as though this was something he saw every day – well the death part is, but not the surroundings I'm sure), then turning to me "Put that woman down. You young people think of nothing but sex. The Reverend can look after her. I need you to give me a hand out with Bob."

We wrapped his poor, frail body in the soft satin sheets (covering his face, to hide that ridiculous ethereal smile that remained frozen on his lips) and the two of us lifted him gently to carry him out to Spankers car. Trying to distract myself from the surreal nature of what we were doing here, I tried to make small talk along the way: "I hadn't realised that you were an Undertaker, Mr Rogers".

"Hmmmph. It's Councillor Rogers actually, Lad...but when we're in here why don't you just carry on calling me "Spanker", like everyone else," and gave me what passed (on him) for a half smile.

Well that told me then! He'll probably bite my head off for the next bit...

"It..It's just that I had a couple of ideas I would like to run by you, if you don't mind..if you've got the time..." I started nervously.

"Bit busy at the moment...catch me tomorrow..." and he grunted as he heaved poor Bob into the boot and slammed down the lid.

Ah well, never mind. He comes here every day. I'd probably be better getting him when he isn't disposing of a dead body anyway. Not the best of times, was it? Besides I've got a little job to finish off in the lock up.

* * *

5 A FIRST TIME

The next day began in a sombre mood. As we sat in the Common Room, sipping on lattés, I allowed the comforting steam to rise up and warm my face. Sabrina similarly was hunched over her cup, the coffee percolating its welcome warm moistness into the pores of her skin and easing the burning in her eyes, reddened and swollen from a sleepless night of constant crying. The death of poor Old Bob, "on the job", had hit us all hard. It had been a shock to everyone, but particularly for Sabrina. Not only had she been his "favourite" (he had been her "once-a-week regular" since the opening of "Blue" – apparently he seemed to think that she in some way resembled his late wife: not I am sure, that his late wife could have possibly have been a Dominatrix), but more importantly that he had actually died under her, at the orgasmic pinnacle of a steamy session of "soixante-neuf".

"Was it me? Did I suffocate him? He would still be alive if it wasn't for me" she sobbed quietly.

"No dear. He was very old. He would have been 94 next birthday. He could've gone at any time," Sapphire tried to console her. "You know he loved you very much. He told me often how much you reminded him of his late wife Emily. She had been gone for several years when he first came to us and he really was not coping at all. He was closer to death then than at any time. You gave him a second lease of life. He would've gone years ago without you. He lived for his little visits, even though it took him a week of sleeping to save up the energy for the next one." At that Sabrina looked up from her cup, a glimmer of a smile on her face, and gave a tiny giggle.

"Do you remember that time when his false teeth got trapped on my nipple ring and fell out?"

They all laughed, and the conversation continued with comical anecdotes recalling the many antics of poor Old Bob, who sounded to have been so accident prone that I could not help but be amazed he had even lived to retirement age, let alone to 93.

Eventually as we chatted, Sapphire caught my eye, and must have prompted her to speak. "So, Tim. What you think of it all after your first week with us? Recent unfortunate events aside, do you think that you would like to stay with us? Perhaps take a more active role even?"

That caught me a little on the hop, and I could not help but to blush, feeling the heat of blood rushing up into my face. "Thank you. It has been....different".
"I'm sure it has," she continued. "I hope you don't mind me saying, but the girls and I had noticed that you do seem to have had a very quiet life up to now."

Where is she going with this? I could feel myself going even redder, gazing down at my feet to check if my laces were still tied.

"Not had a lot of girl friends yet? Been too busy with your studies at the Academy?"

I wriggled in my seat and shuffled my feet, as they wouldn't sit still, coughing as I swallowed my coffee the wrong way, "Hhrrrmmmph!"

"We are very grateful for all your hard work this week, moving our equipment around...and I am also very grateful for how you looked after our little Sabrina yesterday in her hour of need," she continued. "So we thought we would like to give you a little something from us, by way of a "Thank You" gift," and with that she handed me a small, pale blue envelope, personalized with the "Blue" logo inside a circle of tiny red hearts. It felt like a birthday card, or similar inside. All three girls beamed at me as I took it, which I found both puzzling and more than a little bit worrying.

"Thank you. It was my pleasure," I couldn't think of anything more appropriate to say, (although, as I had not yet opened the envelope, I was not sure how appropriate that was or wasn't).

Just at that moment, we were interrupted by the buzzing from the internal telephone (and I was grateful to be off the hook once more). It was Lady Helena who answered the call, apparently from the officer on counter duty. A "lady" had arrived asking for "Miss Harrison", and had been shown into Harry's office to wait for her. She had introduced herself as "Chastity Robinson-Rogers, the leader of the local Temperance group" (and also Chair of the Lady's Flower Arranging Group). She had apparently requested an interview demanding action on "Sleaze."

"Damn! It's Spanker's wife. I'd forgotten she was coming today! I'll have to rush off. Sorry Tim. Catch you later," and at that she hurried off out of the door (and I breathed a healthy sigh of relief at not having to answer any more difficult questions. I didn't want anyone, especially not these girls, finding out that I still hadn't lost my cherry yet at 24 years old).

So now here I was, alone with two very predatory females, both eyeing me up and down as though they had just ordered a takeaway and their next meal had just been delivered. I looked down at the envelope in my hands with a feeling of dread about its contents. They both were obviously in on whatever that was. Lady Helena was the first to speak:

"Go on then! Aren't you going to open it?"

I shuffled in my seat and eyed the envelope some more..

"Shall I help you then?" Lady Sabrina offered.

"No. It's ok. I can manage."

With shaking hands, I tore the end off the envelope and grasped the edge of a gilt edged card. Drawing out the card, I looked down and saw that it was blank.

"Upside down. Turn it over silly" Sabrina giggled. Well, if nothing else it was good to see her laughing again.

Red faced, I turned the card over in my now trembling hands, to see the writing, in beautiful gold calligraphy:

BLUE
Free Taster Session
With a Lady of your Choice

As I stared at the writing on the card, I could hear them both laughing. I felt my neck burning and the heat of my blood rising into my face. Beads of perspiration broke out on my brow and trickled down the sides of my face. It was very strange. I felt burning hot, yet I was shivering. The card shook with the trembling in my hands. This time it was Lady Sabrina who spoke first:

"So which one of us are you going to choose?"
My mouth was dry. So dry that I couldn't speak. I opened my mouth but nothing but a little squeak came out. They were both staring at me as though I was lunch and they hadn't eaten all week. I felt like the victim in one of those vampire movies.

Now I know how a bunny in the headlights really feels.

"So will it be me?" she pressed, reaching out her hand.

They both frighten the pants off me, but it is Sabrina that I really like the most. I would have given anything to have been able to find the courage to ask her out on a date, but I was terrified that she would refuse me and say no. What if she really thought me an idiot? How could I face her every day after that kind of rejection? No.

How could I choose Sabrina? I can barely talk to her, let alone do THAT with her.

Stupidly, I recoiled, taking a step back.

Idiot! Idiot! ID-I-OT!!!!! What the hell are you thinking?

"Ha! I win! It's me then!" Lady Helena wasted no time, jumping up and grasping my tie, dragging me up out of my chair and reeling me in like a prize fish.

Lady Sabrina glared, her eyes flaming like daggers at him. She stamped her foot down, in pique. Then turning for the door, stalked away.

"I'm off! I've got grief counselling with the Reverend anyway. You're welcome to him. Hope it falls off!"

* * *

Lady Helena led me triumphantly by my tie to the Black Room. I had seen it many times before from my vantage point in the control room, but that had been only through the medium of a CCTV monitor. I had never actually been in there, "in the flesh" as it were. What struck me first were the aromas dancing around on my senses, heightened by terror and anticipation: the walnut oil polish on the wood; the mixture of bees wax and orange oil preparations used to keep the leather soft and supple; the herbal side notes from the aroma therapy oils used in massages and spices from unseen incense burners. Soft, ambient music was playing (this time some kind of medieval choir with woodwind accompaniment), originating again from some unseen source, presumably operated by some remote device.

I had seen the monochrome colour scheme through the monitor: with the black flocked walls and the ambient uplighters reflecting in the highly polished floor. What I had never seen on the monitors though was the ceiling. It was fully mirrored: not only reflecting back the light glinting on every piece of polished steel and chrome equipment, but also to allow the "guest" to fully enjoy every angle of enjoyment from their experience.

Dragging me to the centre of the room, she turned and reached up to my neck removing my tie. She drew it through her fingers coiling it around her hand and giving it little testing tugs, murmuring "Hmmm..this has possibilities." Then she turned back to me, ordering me to take off the rest of my clothes, tossing me a fragment of black, leather.

A thong!

"Put that on!"

Stalking over to the wall rack, she ran her fingers along the contents, trailing her long, blood-red nails across each, finally selecting a knotted leather flogger and one other strange object. Despite my terror, I could feel my traitorous erection beginning to stir itself in anticipation.

Then I could see what the other object was that she held in her hand. As she fastened it securely around my neck I saw that it was a studded leather collar, similar to what you would use for a dog, only with two chains hanging from the centre. At end of each chain was a small clamp with sharp metal teeth. She then attached one of each metal clamps to each of my nipples, and I could not help but cry out with the sharp, but erotically sensual pain as the tiny teeth bit into my flesh. She then gave each clamp an extra little twist, just to make me wince once more. Standing back to admire her handiwork she picked up a small riding crop in her right hand and grasping the lead hanging from my collar in her left, she ordered me:

"Down boy!"

Kneeling at her feet on all fours I felt both degraded yet more excited than I had ever experienced in my life, as I anticipated whatever unknown pleasures she might have in store for me. Any pain would be worth that unknown pleasure after the lifetime of frustration I had known up till now. The pain in my nipples was exquisite. It was a sensation like no other I had ever known. They throbbed and pulsated making me aware of every inch of my body and I could feel a rising answering sensation deep down in my groin, as my manhood began to swell.

She led me on all fours across the room to a large, high backed chair. It looked like a throne, but now I was close to it I could see that it was set very low to the ground. I had seen it before on the monitors but had never known what it was for.

"This is a Queening chair. Do you know what we do with it?...No?...You'll soon find out."

She commanded me to lie down on my back with my head under the seat. That was when I noticed that the unusually low seat had a large, round hole cut into it. As I lay there looking up at the ceiling I felt her taking hold of my hands and fastening them in restraints attached to the legs of the chair. Then she sat astride me in the chair, her legs either side of my body, pressing herself into my face.

"Lick me" she commanded, grinding downwards.

I started to lick. Mmmmm, it tasted sweet..yet salty too at the same time, sort of a bit like....

Hmmmm, Marmite? My erection attempts to tear itself out of his thong.. "More, more", she encouraged, cracking the flogger down the sensitive parts of my body; my nipples, the tip of my erection as it was trying to escape its bonds. "Lick my slit" she demanded, through gritted teeth, pressing harder into my face, again licking the flogger off my swollen nipples. "Harder"... then, "lick my clit" she breathed hoarsely, as she ground herself down still deeper onto me in a circular motion, her head thrown back, her long hair cascading down her arching back, her eyes closed, her lips slightly apart. She shuddered, groaning, then almost whispered the command "Stop!"

Tearing at the quick release fastenings on the cuffs, she dragged me out from under the chair and threw me onto the mattress of the bed. "On your back!" she gasped.

Ripping open the ties on my thong, I could feel my erection as it sprang free, as if with a mind of its own. She grasped my manhood roughly and bend to take it fully in her mouth. I could feel the tip as it touched deep into the back of her throat. I did not think anyone could swallow down as deep as that. My eyes were now tightly closed, my cheeks sucked in, my mouth salivating, as I was sure that hers must be also, sweat breaking out on my brow. In a daze I could hear the tearing of a wrapper, and the secondary feeling of loss as she pulled her lips away.

I could smell the aroma of rubber, and of the lubricants of the condom before I even felt it, as she busied herself unrolling it, caressingly, down my throbbing shaft with her deft fingers.

The other strange object was now in her other hand. I could now see that it was some kind of ring, with a device attached, as she grasped my member and forced the object over it.

Straddling my prone body, she forced herself down roughly, impaling herself deep to my hilt, the strange device trapped against her clitoris. Reaching down between her legs she turns it on and I could feel it as it began to vibrate through my entire body. As she rode me roughly, driving herself down on me ever faster and faster, her hands grasped and twisted on the clamps firmly attached to my nipples, sending a feeling like sharp knives down through my body. I could feel the heat rising through my entire body, reaching into my head, my ears burning until I could stand it no more. Then came a feeling like the snapping release of an archer's bowstring as I felt myself explode, pumping my very life's essence into her.

As I lay there spent and exhausted, my face contorted into a stupid smile which spread all over my face, I suddenly felt a feeling of loss as Lady Helena swiftly and professionally dismounted, as though she had done this a million times before.

"Wow! So that's what it's like then? Why the hell was I saving myself!"

* * *

55

6 CHASTITY

Relieved at having gotten rid of the body, I hurried to my office carrying a tray of tea and a plate of cakes. Straightening my dress, and checking my appearance in my reflection in the high gloss of my office door, I paused to tuck an anarchistic wisp of hair securely behind my ear. *It won't do to let that bitch see so much as a chink in my armour!* Opening the door, my poker face now firmly in place, I was confronted by the sight of Chastity Robinson-Rogers seated at my desk in my leather, high-backed rotational chair, swinging herself around from left to right, her hands resting primly on the voluminous handbag firmly across her lap...

"Ahh, Miss Harrison, so glad you were able to join me."

That damn woman. She acts as though this was her office not mine. She has been a thorn in my side for far too long – her and all of that Temperance crap. Here to try to drum up support for her campaign against the brothel again (if only she knew...). She's so far up herself... What she needs is a really good shagging – frustrated old bat! I can't believe she's married to Spanker. He's so damned horny. How can he live with THAT? She's like the Ice Queen. No wonder he's here every day...

Even sitting down you could tell that she was tall (maybe 5'7", or even a bit more); slender but well built. Her light brown hair as always was scraped back into a sharp, bun – so tight that I hoped it was giving her a migraine.

I'll bet there's and impressive figure hidden under those repressive tweed suits and sensible shoes too!

She sat there scrutinising me with those piercing steel blue eyes of hers, pursing her mean, narrow lips in to a condescending smile.

Just look at the state of her, with her badly painted lips, outlined in deep red pencil, but filled in with bright coral-coloured lipstick – has she no idea! And her pasty, pale complexion, all overly-caked in foundation with excessive use of rouge. She looks like a child let loose in Mummy's make up bag! Meeeoww!! Good job I sharpened my claws today. I'm in full-on cat mode.

Resisting the temptation to set the feline free with a catty remark, I set the tray down gently (and as demurely as I could muster) on the desk and took my seat in the moderately smaller and less comfortable chair opposite her (the one that would have been normally designated for guests), inviting her to take tea.

God, I wish I had some cyanide...

Relaxed by the welcome warmth of the tea and no doubt taken in "hook, line and sinker" by my wonderfully "sincere" and inviting nature, she gradually began to relax, eventually chatting away (*yet again, yawn!!*) about her concerns for the town; the alarming growth of sleaze; and the need for "something to be done about it all". I sat there (mentally nitpicking on the state of the chipped varnish on her nails, the nasty, cheap polyester material of her blouse, and 101 other bitchy things I could possibly detect), nodding as "sympathetically" as I thought would appear to be believable (although mentally screwing up everything she says onto imaginary pieces of scrap paper, and tossing them in my mind into a large imaginary waste paper basket) and offered her a bun.

"You must try one of these. They are delicious."

"Oh I really shouldn't"
"Go on. One won't hurt," I cajoled her.
"The ladies of the Women's Institute have been baking

them...Quite hard to get hold of these days. They are quite in demand. They supply them to the Reverend in his tea rooms. Very popular among his outreach groups".

"Aren't you having one?"

No way, José. I know what's in those little bombshells!

"Oh, I've been munching all morning. I'm trying to save myself for later, but you help yourself. Tell me what you think. We'd welcome your suggestions perhaps for other flavours."

I wonder how long it will take for them to take effect? That last stash we sent over looked like it was really good stuff - pretty potent.

I watched with a positively wicked interest as she took a bite, smiling to myself in anticipation of the fun yet to come.

"They are quite an unusual flavour"

"Yes they are Mrs Fotherington's secret herbal recipe. Apparently came from her mother."

As we chatted on, Chastity continued to nibble away on the bun, absent-mindedly reaching for another, then another. As time passed, she eventually reached for the last bun.

"Oh dear, they are rather more-ish aren't they?"

I'll bet they are! That'll be "the Munchies" setting in...

"Don't worry, there's plenty more, and they are very low calorie," I forced a smile at her.

However, chatting on, under the ever increasing influence of the Herbal cakes, I began to wonder if I hadn't perhaps treated her a little unkindly. She was beginning to grow on me. I was gradually revising my opinion of her. As she relaxed, she admitted to her feelings of repression. The tight-laced, prudish, repressed front was just her means of protection from letting the world know her true, secret desires. She told me how she had long regretted that her husband was too boring to indulge in any of her fantasies.

If only she knew Councillor Rupert Rogers the way we did!

Eventually as the cakes kicked in properly, the little secret "herbal" extras, melting into her bloodstream, she started to giggle, recounting to me all the fantasy thoughts that now began to reappear in her mind, after having been forcibly kept dormant all of these years: thoughts of what she would like to have done with her boring husband, had he not been a respectable town councillor.

This poor girl has suffered for quite long enough. I think it is our womanly duty to help her...

Considering her now well-inebriated state, she was obviously ready for a bit of fun. I had originally just intended letting her sleep it off and then send her home later in a taxi, but now I thought we should really take this a bit further. She was in drastic need of a "makeover".

While she had been chatting and I had been sitting facing her, I had, while covered by the desk, without her noticing removed my sensible office court shoes and replaced them. My legs were now covered from thigh to ankle by a pair of skin tight, black, wet-look boots, terminating in narrow pointed feet, tipped in ornate silver sheaths.

I stood, raising myself to my full height on my 6 inch silver needle-like stiletto heels, unfastening the belted waist of my navy silk shirt-dress.

"We have been watching you for some time, you saucy little Minx. I think it's about time you joined us."

At that I drew open the Velcro closure of my cross-over fronted dress, shrugging it off my shoulders backwards, and let it fall loosely to the chair behind me, revealing my alter-ego, "Madame Sapphire".

At my neck I wore a narrow, black-studded choker. Below that I wore a black, burlesque-style corset, trimmed with electric blue lace; similar lace picking out the strongly-boned structure of its panelling; and decorated in places by tiny blue jewels, which seem to flash in reflection of the subdued lighting as I moved. I had deliberately chosen the tightness of the corset's extreme lacing to fully extenuate the extremes of my figure: my full, rounded hips, my narrow waist and my scarcely-contained heaving breasts. The corset had two different means of access: it was fastened at the front by a series of shining steel hooks (studs inserted through sliding steel loops); but at the back it was drawn in by two sets of criss-crossing satin laces. One lace started at the top; the other started at the base; meeting in the centre where it was drawn in tightly and secured in a bow, to create a most extreme waist narrowing. Below the corset I matched it with a black silk thong, also trimmed with electric blue lace. To complete the *"ensemble"*, suspenders reached down from the corset, across the flawless porcelain skin of my upper thigh, clasped to my shining black stockings.

It was a shame that she was too far gone to fully experience the hard work that had gone into producing this *"magnus opus"*, and an even bigger shame that she would probably not even remember much of it tomorrow.

Taking Chastity by the hand, I led her (heavily under the influence of the Herbal cakes), through to the Black Room, where Timothy was still resting after his little "encounter" with Lady Helena. He was now however, more appropriately dressed as a "Bondage Master", having successfully passed his "initiation" into our little "team". Lady Helena had surpassed herself, dressing him in black leather boxer shorts, which really showed off his impressive package (who would have thought that such a quiet, unassuming young man would have been so well endowed?). The strength of the effect of his appearance lay in its simplicity: bold, yet slightly understated: his only accessories being a pair of black leather, studded wristbands. He was reclining seductively on the blood-red leather mattress of the impressive king-sized bed, casually rapping across his palm with a short riding crop.

At the sight of him, Chastity smiled, giggling again like a teenager on heat:

"Oooh, he's pretty, isn't he?"

"Would you like him to join us, Chastity?" I invited, holding out my hand towards this vision of rippling muscles and raging testosterone before us.

She nodded, blushing and giggling once more, like an embarrassed school girl.

"From now on, in here you must call me "Mistress" and he will be "Master". Do you understand?"

She giggled once more

"Yes, Mistress."

Taking her by the hand I led her across to the bed, pressing on her shoulders to sit her down on the edge. Leaning forward, I was drawn to the burning heat of her lips, and was gratified to feel them part for me, inviting my probing tongue access to explore the moisture of her mouth. Through the fog that seemed to deaden her thoughts, her mind told her that this must be wrong, to be kissing another woman. But it felt so nice, and a soft, soothing voice in her ear (my voice) kept pressing her that "there is nothing to be ashamed of in your own body", that "if something gives you pleasure, then it must be good", to "just go with your feelings" and "to just lie back and enjoy it". Clearly, she was not just enjoying it; she was positively relishing it; as she responded demonstrably to my advances.

Tim then joined us, placing a blindfold over her eyes, darkening her world, leaving her alone with her senses.

* * *

Chastity could feel the breath of somebody close, against her skin;

and she was sure that she could feel more than one pair of hands caressing her body, slowly unfastening her clothing and freeing her body from their restraints. She could smell the aromas of the room, of leather and of a honey-like beeswax polish, mixed with citrus undertones, She ran her hands down the side of her body, over the leather mattress of the bed, until she felt the close-cropped hair of the young man beside her. She could also pick out the clean aroma of soap and the muskiness of his body, along with faint traces of his aftershave. As she continued to run her hands through his hair, she pondered on how soft it feels, like a little mole. Then feeling his breath on her inner thighs, she realised that he was between her now open legs...but the feeling was so nice, so relaxing, "there can be nothing wrong with this" as the voice had told her. He was now nuzzling down deeper between her legs, but she could also feel another mouth on her breasts, twirling her nipple with its tongue and nibbling gently with its teeth. Although there was pain, it was a warm, tingling feeling at the same time. There was no way that she wanted it to stop.

Down below again, and she could feel his tongue exploring her lips, the entrance to her sex, and entering inside her gently in a swirling motion. Then he trailed back up, towards her button, licking and swirling.

She felt within her an awakening....of something long dormant.

This was something alien to her, yet at the same time familiar. It reminded her of many, many years before...with her husband, before they were married, before he was pulled into working for his father in the undertaking business. It was a time when he was carefree and attentive, and when they were so happy. But even then, it was never like this. He was always so shy, so polite. How she had longed sometimes that he would just cast respectability to the wind and just take her. But no he waited.

Then they married and it all changed.

This was how she had always hoped he would be.

She felt her hips start to move in a rhythmical motion as his tongue continued to work on her in a circular motion; her cheeks clenching as her hips tilted forward into him; she felt the blood rise inside her, flushing into her face, her ears burning; and she felt almost as though she would explode.

Then he stopped!

She was bereft

.

Then she felt his hands once more. He turned her over, grasping her ankles and dragging her to the edge of the bed; her legs hanging down over the edge as though she were kneeling. Gentle hands now forced her cheeks apart. Fingers were trailing, cold, with some kind of liquid between her cheeks, then gently pushing their way inside her...into a place where no-one had ever probed before. Then the fingers withdrew and were replaced by something cold and harder. It reached down deeper inside her than the fingers had done before.

There was a "click" and a buzzing, vibrating feeling, started up deep down inside her. Whatever it was inside her, it was now moving, sending shocks through her body.
The strong hands rolled her body back over again. She could feel as his tongue was once more upon her, trailing down from her belly button, towards her lower lips.

"Yes, yes Master. Please" she begged, desperate for him not to stop.

Then she heard a tearing sound and could detect a faint aroma of sweet, fruit flavoured lubricant and latex, followed by the sound of a condom unrolling.

Her mind leapt in anticipation as she imagined his beautiful shaft – swollen, engorged, and ready just for her.

Suddenly he was on top of her. She could feel him at her entrance, tentatively deliberating, teasing her – then in one sudden move, he entered her, thrusting deeper than she ever imagined possible.

"Yes!" she screamed.

"Take me!"

He began to pound into her, thrusting rhythmically deeper and deeper; and she could feel his full length forcing itself against the end of her. He was as deep as it was possible for anyone, or anything to ever reach. .At the same time she could feel the vibrations of the object deep inside her, taking her to still more pleasure from behind.

This was what she had been waiting for all these years - what she had been deprived of while Rupert had been out at all of those meetings; and in her head she fantasized that it was him inside her thrusting ever deeper.

The blood rushed to her head once more. Her ears burned. She felt as though she would explode. Could she take much more of this? Again, she felt the other hands upon her breasts, pulling and twisting at her nipples once more, then touching her with a vibrating wand that sent electric shocks down through both of her breasts.

She could take no more and screamed with her every fibre, as she felt his entire body shudder and release himself into her.

Then he relaxed and slid gently out of her, reaching down and removing the vibrator from her anus. Crawling up her exhausted body, he kissed her burning lips passionately, his tongue reaching deep down into her throat.

"Thank you, Chastity," his voice whispered softly in her ear, as he removed the blindfold.

The world felt warm and safe. Everything passed into a red blur around her and she fell into a deep sleep, partly through ecstatic exhaustion and partly through the effects of all of the herbal cakes she had consumed.

* * *

7 AN UN-NATURAL LOSS

Leaving Chastity to sleep it off in the Black Room, we had barely had time to sit ourselves down with a warm welcoming cup of frothy latte when we were interrupted once more by the buzzing from the internal telephone. Yet again it was the officer on counter duty, reporting the arrival of a "male person" for "Miss Harrison" (the rather bland terminology alerting me to the suggestion that the person may have been of a more "suspicious" nature). The lack of name, or rank, indicated that this call was not related to Police business. It was clearly not an official visit, nor was it any scheduled interviewee. The person had been shown into one of the two small private interview rooms set to the side of the front counter and directed to take a seat (again he had not been shown into my office, as had been the case with Chastity, suggesting that this person may not be trustworthy).

The hairs on the back of my neck stood up. I couldn't put my finger on it, but something was not right. Changing back into my "Harry" persona (smart, navy-blue office dress and sensible shoes), after suggesting to Tim that he should monitor the situation on the CCTV, I headed cautiously for the interview room and my mysterious, unannounced guest.

Each of the two interview rooms were identical. They were sparsely decorated, with plain, pale blue walls, white ceiling and dark grey carpeting (as would be typical for any budget office purposes). The room had no window and was illuminated only by harsh fluorescent tube lighting overhead. On the opposite side to the door through which an interviewee would have entered, there was a second door, allowing access through from the Station's central corridor. In the centre of the room, against one wall, there was a plain, unremarkable pine table with three chairs, one facing for interviewer use, and the two closest for use by the interviewee and their representative. On the table stood a long, rectangular tape recorder, with openings on the front designed to accommodate three tapes simultaneously.

When I opened the door from the central corridor, the arrogant toad was directly ahead of me. He was a mountainous, gorilla of a man – aged about 40, tall and muscular with greenish-brown eyes, swarthy olive skin, a narrow moustache and a neatly trimmed goatee beard. The room was filled with the aroma of the fragrant, musk-based oil which he obviously used to slick his shining, black hair back to his head. Overall he gave a Mediterranean appearance, although that was belied as soon as he spoke by his London (possibly "Cockney") accent. With his "chav-tastic" style of expensive but tasteless "designer" fashions (sharp suit and Italian shoes), his appearance screamed out with every inch of him, exactly what he was: a Pimp (and probably a very successful one looking at the price of his suit)!

He was sitting stretched out on one of the opposing seats, his arms raised, his neck resting on his hands. He was leaning back in his chair, with his legs crossed at the ankles, and resting on the edge of the table, as though he owned the place. I was hoping that he would lean too far and crash down on the floor, although I knew in my heart I would be disappointed by that wish.

This is some kind of power game he's playing here.

Pretending not to notice, I forced myself to display my most captivating and enticing smile, sashaying into the seat directly facing him, and deliberately crossing my legs to "accidentally" reveal a generous amount of inner thigh.

"So how can I help you today, Mr.......erm?" prompting him for an introduction.

With that, he sat up slowly, leaning forwards on his elbows and crossing his fingers tightly, the whiteness of his knuckles being an obvious "tell" to his true displeasure (along with a slight narrowing of his eyes and an almost imperceptible tick to his left eye). Expecting that I would have known (and been suitably impressed and intimidated), he introduced himself with insincere politeness, as Vinnie "the Knife" Laffitte, the owner of a "similar" establishment in the neighbouring city, adding that he was "taking over" our operations and that he had come to "check out the facilities".

Trailing one hand down the side of his face, outlining lightly with my finger a deep scar running down his right cheek, I looked directly into his eyes and smiled deeply at him.

"Oh, I'm so glad you have come. Why don't we slip into my special room and have a nice little drink to celebrate." Then taking him by the hand I led him down the corridor to my dungeon, the Blue Room.

The Blue Room was very much similar to the other two (belonging to Lady Sabrina and Lady Helena). It had the same high level, soft-glowing ambient lighting, although with a polished mahogany floor, a plain black ceiling, and deep royal-blue coloured softly flocked walls. The room was also filled with similar aromas of orange and walnut oils, and beeswax polish for the wooden and leather fittings. The fixtures and fittings in general were similar also, with a luxurious king-sized bed (with satin sheets), a chest of drawers, and a wall rack of canes and whips. At the end of the room it also featured a tall, high-backed Queening chair and a large wooden wheel device fitted with cuffs for wrists and ankles.

In the centre of the room, towards the wall with the door, was a solid wooden table and a couple of matching stools. Placing a bottle of red wine and two glasses on the table I invited him to take a seat. Then stretching my arms out wide, as though pretending to be tired, I opened my gown and cast it aside on the bed, seating myself just out of reach from him, on the opposite stool. Lifting one foot, dressed in a black, wet-look laced up boot, with a 6 inch silver heel, I rested it playfully in his crotch.

He gazed incredulously at my body, barely contained by my black, wet-look shiny latex cat-suit, deliberately left open at the inner thighs and crotch. The bodice was fronted by a wide, plunging neckline, exposing both of my heaving breasts, their size extenuated by a corseted waist cincher, or "waspie", formed in similar material to the cat-suit, but decorated with long conical silver studs. At my neck I was wearing a narrow, black-studded choker, two silver chains passing from its centre to each breast. I could see in his eyes how they were magnetically drawn to these chains, following their route from neck to breast, and in particular where they terminated in large, silver rings piercing each nipple.

I've got him!

Extending an arm covered in a full length wet-look glove, I purposefully picked up and fondled the corkscrew, before inserting it into the bottle, turning the screw and slowly extracting the cork. I then placed the cork between my lips and sucked on it, placing it on the table beside the glasses. Pouring us both a glass of the wine, I dipped my finger into one, rubbing the wine around my pouting lips, which glistened and shone under the subdued lighting. Leaning across the table towards Vinnie, I repeated the same with him, moistening his lips with the wine. I watched as he licked his lips hungrily, biting at the bait. Then lifting the other glass, swirling the contents slowly, I passed it to him, taking the first glass for myself.

In my most sultry voice I purred, "The ladies and I just want to be free to enjoy our work. They are all very dedicated to the services we offer. We are quite bored with all of the business side of things these days. It just distracts us from our real vocation."

Then, stroking lightly down his chest and fingering slowly one of his already hardening nipples, I invited him, "Wouldn't you like to try out our services before you agree to become our new protector."

"We can provide a range of personal services to our guests, either simple "vanilla", or based on any fantasy that you have in mind. We even have a selection of ready-made scenarios to allow them to "taste" a sample of what we have to offer: we have "classroom days with teacher"; "Mummy and Baby"; or perhaps a selection of fairy stories - "Little Bo Peep", "Pussy in Boots", "Goldilocks", just to name a few."

Standing, I crossed around to his side of the desk, and perching one cheek on the corner, next to his raised feet I lightly twirled the laces of his shoes absent-mindedly with my fingers. Closing my eyes for a second as I licked my full, slightly-parted glistening lips, I continued:

"Although the "specialité" of the house here really is BDSM.
We like both to give and to receive."

Reaching forward and trailing my long fingers down each of the buttons of his shirt, deftly and professionally "popping" each open on passing, I purred in his ear, "Do you have any preference for either today?"

My fingers continued on their journey, trailing the line formed by the hairs on his stomach down towards the waistband of his trousers, making him shudder in anticipation. Flicking open the top button, I released the pressure formed by his ever expanding erection pressing against the fabric, forcing the zip to slowly creep open under its own control.

"No?" I continued, as the zipper reached that point of no return, when his erection sprang proud. I let out a small gasp of faked appreciation at my success, breathing in deeply as I once more allowed my tongue to run around my lips, biting lightly on the bottom lip and whispering breathlessly, "Then we will have to try a selection of both".

"Come" I groaned, grasping the front of his shirt and peeling it off backwards. Then swiftly I relieved him of his trousers.

Casting aside my gown, I then revealed myself to him in full

Dominatrix costume:

Taking him lightly by the hand I led him across to the Queening chair, taking my seat in it. "Cuff me into the chair," I commanded softly. As he had been directed, he took each of my hands and secured them in the restraints on each arm of the chair (without realising that although meant to be in the "Submissive" role, I was still in fact acting strongly but passively as the "Dominant"). "And my ankles too!" I directed, pointing at him with the shining silver tip on my black, wet-look boots.

"Now lie down between my feet, with your head under the seat!"
I waited while he assumed the position, "and lick me until I scream for mercy."

As his tongue began to explore the most sensitive parts of my body, I responded by pressing down further onto his face, grinding in a circular motion. As the intensely pleasurable sensations took hold of me, I allowed myself to explore visually the muscular body of this powerful adversary whom I had just skilfully debased before me. "Harder.. harder!" I gasped, my eyes taking in the many scars, testament to the many battles that had no doubt earned him his title of "The Knife". "He would be a strong ally to have on your side, but a terrible and unforgiving enemy", I thought to myself. I would have to be very careful here to keep him under control, or the results could be devastating..... although the experience could be immensely pleasurable too...."

My mind had almost begun to drift into the torturous and sensual ecstasy of his ever probing tongue, when I managed to snap myself back into control.

"Enough! Stop, stop!" I gasped.

Snapping the hidden quick release on each of the cuffs, then bending down to repeat on each ankle, I rose and stepped over his prone body towards the chest of drawers.

"My turn now!"...."Come here!"

Desperate now for sexual release (and as pliable as putty in my hands), he followed me to the chest. "Put these on!" I commanded, throwing him a glossy black latex thong with heavily studded leather codpiece. As he straightened up, to pull the thong into place, I ran my hands down his chest, exploring the contours and feeling at the many healed scars with appreciation. "Magnificent!" I whispered.

Reaching into one of the drawers I pulled out two pairs of studded leather cuffs, snapping first the smaller pair around his wrists, then bending over to snap the larger set around his ankles, As I rose, I took great care to deliberately rub my heaving breasts against his abdomen and chest, making him suck in his breath in anticipation. I swirled my tongue around one nipple, nuzzled across the valley of his chest and swirled my tongue around the other nipple, nibbling it lightly with my teeth, forcing both to harden and stand proud.

Then reaching up I pulled down two chains from an iron track way above me, clipping one to each of his wrist restraints.
"Raise your arms!" I commanded, and he complied without question, his chest rising and falling with frustrated sexual tension.
Stepping to the side of the chest, my hand fell on a polished bronze wheel.

Suddenly spinning the wheel, his arms were pulled out to each side, chaining him securely in the centre of the room.

"Now open your legs!" I directed him, adding. "This is going to be the best thing you will have ever experienced," and clipped his ankles to each end of a long, stainless steel spreader bar.
"Almost ready," as I reached up and pulled a black latex mask over his head, zipping it up closed from behind. The mask had a large round hole for the mouth and two smaller holes for the nose. From these, two small tubes extended.

"The whole experience will be heightened by the sensory deprivation of being blindfolded by the mask, forcing you to turn your awareness of your senses inwards. Touch and feeling will be magnified to compensate....like this," and with that I reached across and nipped once more on his nipple, making him gasp.

"Are you enjoying it?" I asked.

"Oh, yes" he replied, at which he received a sharp slap on his behind.

"Yes Mistress is the correct response when you are here in my world, thank you!

Now, once more. Are you enjoying it?" I asked.

"Yes, thank you Mistress," he replied and I felt my mouth curl up into a wide, lascivious smile.

"Just one more thing and it'll be perfect," I added, drawing from the chest a short fabric belt, with a round ball in the middle. "Open wide. I have something special for you."

He opened his mouth wide, in anticipation of something good about to happen. Instead I thrust the ball into his mouth, clipping the belt tightly around the back of his head.

"There! You are all done. Now I'll show you what we do with naughty little boys."

Crossing to the wall rack of canes and whips, I selected the monster of all – the "Cat of nine tails". Standing behind him to his left, my legs slightly apart, I raised the "Cat" in my right hand and brought it down swiftly and firmly across his back, the "tails" biting into his flesh, leaving a long, pale gash, darkening to deep red by the second. Quickly I followed this by a second and then a third strike across his buttocks.

Vinnie strained on the chains holding his wrists, trying to twist and turn to avoid the blows, but to no avail. He was securely restrained and unable to get away – unable even to anticipate the next blow due to the blackness of his hood. His eyes blazed with hatred as he realised that he has been tricked.

There was a brief respite where the flogging stopped, and he wondered what was happening, but I had only crossed back to the chest, taking various small objects from the drawers, replacing the "Cat" in the rack and selecting a new "weapon" – this time a short whip.

Then he heard the click of my 6 inch metal heels on the polished floor as I returned, then a short delay followed by even more intense pain, first this time across his nipples and then across his scrotum, as the whip struck. Then he felt hands upon his body, my fingers probing deep into his anus. He tried to buck away, but there was no escape. Then the fingers withdrew, for just a second, to be followed by something hard, metallic and unforgiving. He heard a click, followed by a buzzing sound, simultaneous with an intensely hot, burning agony in his anus. His chest heaved, he felt his heart racing as though it was exploding within his chest. He tried to scream but no noise escaped past the ball in his mouth. Then blackness.

With his lifeless body now lying there limp, the threat to us all had evaporated away along with his life. I called through to Tim for assistance, as though there had been a terrible accident. In floods of well-rehearsed crocodile tears, I told him that Vinnie had gone too far in his session and had choked to death in his gimp mask, although I was not quite sure from his expression whether he fully believed me - whether it was an accident or did I do it deliberately?"

Either way, it doesn't matter. The end justifies the means. He was a vicious psychopath and would have killed us all if I hadn't done something.

We were probably going to need the skills of Spanker once more to help us to dispose of the body (dead people being his speciality, although strictly speaking only usually those who died of natural or accidental causes). In the meantime, I stood there contemplating the dead pimp and the possible consequences.

After a few minutes of contemplation however, a solution came to mind that would solve one other problem - Chastity. I explained to Tim how we've already got CCTV filming of her with me and him earlier. We can also use the pimp here to get some more material on her as well, editing in the best bits later. He wasn't too convinced though. He seemed to think it was a bit too perverse, but he went along with it any way.

Tim helped me to redress the dead pimp in a leather crotch

harness, fitted with a large black rubber dildo, of a type normally worn by dominant women. We then disguised the harness by dressing him in a pair of zip-fronted black leather shorts, unzipped to allow its black rubber member to spring free, as though imbued with a life of its own. Then carrying the dead pimp across to the Queening chair and sitting him in it, we strapped his ankles to its legs, fastening his wrists behind his back with zip ties, his large black member standing proud. The sight of him was both absolutely ridiculous, and yet terrifyingly alive. However, his cold dead eyes still stared out at me.

Placing a full black leather mask on his head which fully covered his eyes and mouth, with just two small holes for the nose, he looked more alive (and could no longer stare at me accusingly). Finally, strapping his head to the high back of the chair with a broad leather strap across his forehead stopped his head from lolling over to one side.

Returning to the Black Room we collected the now very drowsy Chastity, shaking her to wake up. Fixing a leather collar and lead to Chastity, Tim then led her on all fours into centre of the Blue room, directly in line with the cameras. He then ordered her to open his cod piece, encouraging her by flicking her across her behind and nipples with a soft suede flogger. As his now engorged member sprung free, he ordered her to take it in her mouth and suck. When she felt his familiar shaft in her mouth she smiled and roused herself, sucking on him so greedily that it made him gasp.

"Wow! You really want it don't you?" he ask her.
She nodded insatiably.

"Beg for it" he commanded her.

At that, she raised her head, his manhood deep into her throat, looking longingly into his eyes and raised her hands as though begging to him. He then stepped back, pulling out of her mouth, leaving her empty and desolate.

"Let's see just how much you can take, you greedy girl. Crawl to the chair!" he barked.

Then, taking her lead in his hand, he directed her across to the dead pimp.

"Take him in your mouth now," he ordered.

At his command, she crouched over the prone pimp, taking his rubber length fully into her mouth without realising the deception, and started to suck.

Approaching her from behind, Tim then raised up her legs, which he forced apart, while pressing her head further down into the pimp's lap. Reaching down between her legs, into the warmth of her sex, he forced two fingers deep inside her, probing around inside until she groaned aloud in pleasure.

"How wet you are!" He exclaimed. "You are really ready for it aren't you?" Then removing his fingers he aligned himself and thrust his manhood deep inside her, making her cry out with the fullness of him. Gripping her hair with one hand and reaching around for her breast with the other, seizing her nipple tightly, he thrust in and out, over and over, shouting "suck him you bitch! Harder! Harder!" Then with a shudder, he exploded inside her.

"Enough!" he shouted, and Chastity slumped once more to the floor, curling up into a ball and passing out at his feet. Tim then picked her up and carried her back to the Black room, where he laid her gently on the bed, asleep.

* * *

8 CLEANING UP

We seemed to be having a most bizarre run of bad luck. I had wondered what I was getting myself into here, whether I should have just run a mile in the opposite direction when I first met Madame Sapphire. This was the second fatality in less than a week. This can't be normal. If we lost punters at that rate all the time, there wouldn't be anyone left in the town by now. No, it must just be a pure fluke. Poor Old Bob had been just waiting to go for decades, ever since his wife passed on before him. He could have popped off just watching an exciting episode of Gardener's World. At least he went with a smile on his face.

But now we have a second body to get rid of. That last one was really strange. He was only relatively young (perhaps in his early forties), and built like a "brick shit house". He had muscles on his muscles. I wouldn't have liked to come across him in a dark alleyway. He looked like he had survived no end of street fights in his rather dubious career – not the sort of man that you would expect to "pop off" in the throes of passion. Still, off he had popped after all. There was no getting around that one.

I suppose Madame Sapphire was probably right. He could have had a "dicky ticker" or something in his head that popped without warning. You do hear of it happening in quite young, athletic people. But we could hardly call out a doctor for a full autopsy could we? We can't even let anyone know he had been here at all.

It had to be kept quiet and sweep everything under the carpet. At least, if anyone missed him (which I would doubt), the Police Station has got to be the absolute last place on Earth that anyone would be likely to come looking for him. What's more, as we would be the ones investigating the disappearance of any missing persons, we would be unlikely to find any traces of his visit. We know every trick in the book about how to hide the evidence.

No. One thing is certain. No matter what else, there is absolutely no way that Sapphire (or any of the girls for that matter), could have had anything to do with his death. It was my duty to help protect them from public scrutiny, and from any suspicion of wrong-doing...especially my Sabrina!

I had already been busy this morning, setting things in motion to sort out Sabrina's other little problem – Sergeant Tosser! Tonight I would "fix" him for good. We'll soon be rid of him.

Last night I had rung the top hotel in town, the Grand Empire Hotel, and booked a room in Tosser's name. Then I bought a bottle of champagne and borrowed a few things off the girls to finish things off: a skimpy baby-doll nightdress, lipstick and some sleeping pills. Finally I'd texted Tosser (or maybe that should've been "sex-ted" him?), as Sabrina to meet her at the hotel at 9pm (guessing that it should be dark by 8pm).

This morning I'd been to the Hotel early and checked in on one of those automatic check-in systems to get the room keys, using the credit card I had temporarily "borrowed" from Tosser's locker (*well there is no way I'm going to use my money for this am I? It's going to cost him a small fortune*). Then, climbing the backstairs to the room, so not to be seen, I had checked out the room for the best view, and set up a tiny, covert CCTV camera, taking the receiver into the bathroom to check out the image. It was perfect. You could see everything in the room.

But that was this morning. Everything had seemed to be going like clockwork, but now I was not so sure. Sapphire was busy on her mobile to Spanker, asking him to come back to collect "another one". If anyone can help us to get rid of a dead body, an undertaker is the ideal person.

"No, don't bring the hearse. Not in your undertaker's outfit. This one has to be even quieter than the last one. I'll explain when you get here. Just come as you would for any usual visit."

She heaved a deep sigh as she pressed the "end call" button, tucking her mobile 'phone safely back into the elasticated garter belt around her upper thigh – Spanker was on his way. With things now heading in the right direction; a plan beginning to come together; disposal of the body underway; a wave of calm and clarity washed over her and she visibly relaxed back into her usual air of command. She was back in control and ready for whatever came her way next.

Resting her chin on her thumb and forefinger, she pondered aloud, "The next job will be to dispose of that horrendous "Pimp-mobile" parked in the dark alleyway behind the station. That won't be easy. It's hardly what you could call inconspicuous, is it? We also need to get rid of Chastity. We can't let Spanker see her in that state when he gets here. Do you think you could take care of that please, Tim?

Taking Chastity home would be easy enough. I would just need to pour her into bed when we get there. She was not wrong about that car though. It wouldn't be an easy one to dispose of. Certainly it can't be found anywhere too near here, but as long as it is wiped clean, and isn't found for some time, they shouldn't be able to tie it to us. The man was in a dodgy line of work, so nobody will be too surprised that he disappears eventually. It's an occupational hazard. The same would apply to his motor. I just have to make sure there's no trail back to us and delay its discovery.

One thing is pretty damned obvious though. I can't do it dressed like this!

Glancing down, I realized I was still wearing my leather Bondage Master outfit; all black leather and studs. That won't do! Nor could I be seen in my uniform. Anyone who saw me might not see my face under my helmet, but the uniform would be immediately recognisable as a Police Officer. I needed to change first.

Dressing hurriedly in my civilian clothes (thankfully I have been going through a "black" theme lately, possibly reflecting my fascination with the dungeons and all of that "dark" equipment", so my civvies consisted of black, tightly fitting turtle-neck sweater and black denim jeans), I half carried the drowsy Chastity out through the back door of the station, across to the recently orphaned "pimp-mobile" waiting in the dark, lonely alleyway behind. She staggered alongside me, her arms draped around my neck; hopefully with the intention that if anyone had spotted us they would have just thought us a pair of drunken lovers, a little too worse for pair after an evening out on the lash. Reaching the car however, I was in a quandary - how to unlock the car without relaxing my grip on Chastity? There was no way around it. I needed at least one hand free.

As I released my hold on her to unlock the car door with the remote, her knees buckled and she slid down my front, giggling. Then she raised her arms to pull herself back up, placing her hand on my crotch and fingering my zip.
With slurring words, she asked "Shall I give you a blow job here in the street, big boy?"

Swatting her hands away quickly before anyone saw her, I managed to pull her back up onto her feet "Not just now, thanks." With that, I opened the rear passenger side door and poured her in across the back seat.

No time to mess with seat belts just this once. Nobody will see her down there.

Crossing to the driver's door I opened it and slid into the soft, luxurious leather bucket seats, behind the steering wheel which was dressed in a soft, padded goatskin cover. The car was top of the range, with polished walnut controls and full leather upholstery. The aroma of new car and freshly oiled leather tempted my senses. How I had dreamt of driving in a car like this for just once in my life. It was like a fantasy come true.

What a shame it will be such a short fantasy. It will be a crime to have to dispose of this car.

I laughed to myself at that thought:
A crime?
As if murder isn't a crime?
Get over yourself. It's just a damn car!
Damn good job nobody can hear me arguing with myself...

I started the engine and the car immediately responded, purring to life. It really was like a living animal, and a powerful one too.

Driving through the centre of town, how I wished that people could see me at the wheel of this car, fantasizing that I was some kind of rock star, footballer or multi-millionaire playboy, while at the same time hoping to God that nobody recognised me. Eventually, approaching Chastity's house, in the quiet, tree-lined road in the more well-heeled part of town, I turned into the wide gravelled driveway and killed the engine, coasting silently to a halt outside the door.

Lifting the sleeping Chastity from the back of the car (trying my utmost not to waken her again), tapping the door gently shut with my foot, I carried her into the safety of the silent, empty house.

At least I managed to get us that far without having her tear my clothes off in the street!

In the first floor master bedroom, I laid her gently on the white satin spread covering the king-sized bed, next to a giant fluffy teddy bear. This was a strange thing to find in an adult, married woman's room. I couldn't see many men wanting to share their pride of place "in bed with a Ted". Glancing around the room now with fresh eyes, it was apparent that all was not as it seemed in Councillor Roger's marriage. I couldn't help but notice how everything I saw belonged to Chastity, with nothing belonging to Spanker anywhere in sight.

He obviously sleeps elsewhere! This is her private haven. He probably never even visits.

As she realised that I was no longer holding her, she roused slightly, lifting her arms once more to caress my body. Then, reaching the waistband of my trousers, she began to slide down my zipper, freeing the wakening beast within once more. "You don't seem to be in such a hurry now", she purred sleepily, grasping my man-toy and pulling me towards her, as she bit down lightly on her bottom lip. At first I tried to resist (although I must admit, I wasn't trying too, hard):

What a Cougar! This girl is insatiable...

Then, feeling that now familiar feeling sparking back to life, deep down below my waist:

"Oh, what the hell. Her husband won't be back for hours and it's too light outside to get rid of the car yet......"

* * *

With darkness now settled on the world, and after thoroughly wiping it clean of any finger prints, I pulled away from the house in the powerful monster of a car, heading towards the sea lake, down by the beach. A plan had half formed in my head while I had been biding away my time so pleasurably with Chastity. I had considered driving the car into the lake and letting it rot, but then now as I thought about it, I worried that there was too much chance of it being found. Fishermen often sit around the edge, trying to catch the many flatties that live on the lake bottom. What if their lines caught on the wreckage? I would need to get the car deeper out into the water. But how?

At one end of the lake there was a construction site, where the rides of the disused fairground were being demolished and taken away for scrap. The demolition machinery sat eerily abandoned in the darkness: amongst them, a giant crane resembled some kind of ancient dinosaur. I pulled the car up just in front of it, next to the water's edge. Releasing the hook from the front of the machine, I attached it under the sill at the front of the car.

Climbing up into the cab of the dinosaur/crane, I turned the key in the ignition, awakening the monster, and pulling the lever to raise the arm. The beautiful limousine groaned as it raised up by its front end, the cable creaking under its weight. Then it lifted clear off the ground, swinging there in front of me.

I spun the large wheel controlling the arm of the beast, swinging the car out deep over the black body of water. As I once more lowered the arm, bringing the car down towards the water, my burden reaches its maximum distance from the lake edge. I could hear the water breaking around the body of the car as it sank down below the surface. Then I pressed the lever to release the hook, the arm springing clear as it was freed from the weight. The car then slid almost silently down to the bottom of the lake (silent that is, apart from a lapping of the water and the sound of escaping bubbles from air trapped within the body).

After returning the crane to its original sleeping position, I set off on foot back towards the station. It was freezing cold in the night air, but still, I felt warm with the excitement and fear of discovery. I also felt hot with excitement as I recalled my "adventures of the day", both in the Black Room, and later in Chastity's bed.

I think I'm going to like this new job.

But the day was not yet over. It was 7pm. I had to get myself to the hotel for 8pm and I still had some things to collect

* * *

That evening, I returned to the hotel at 8pm in the dog-handler's van, parking around the back, in the back street. Putting the backpack over my shoulder, I opened the back doors of the van. "Come on Flossie".

This time both Flossie and I climbed silently up the back stairs to the room. Thankfully nobody saw us.

"Right Flossie, you go in the bathroom and get ready, while I see to the room"

So, then I got busy. I laid out a pink baby-doll nightie trimmed in virginal snowy white fluffy fur on the bed cover. Next I sprinkled rose petals around on the floor, setting out a bottle of champagne and two glasses on dressing table, with a card next to the bottle. In beautiful cursive script on the card it said:

Just having a little bath.
Have a few drinkies while you wait to get in the mood.
I'll be ready for you soon lover boy!!
Xxx (kisses on the bottom)

In the corner of the card was a big, bright red lipstick kiss. The perfect finishing touch! Then, opening the bottle, I crushed several sleeping tablets and dissolved them into the contents, swirling it around to help them melt away, and sent another text to Tosser:

"Hurry up lover boy, I'm lay on the bed, burning for your hot body. May have to have a cool bath to calm myself down if you don't get here soon. xxx"

Then I headed for the bathroom to turn on the monitor.
"Are you ok in there Flossie? Time to get ready."

Back in the bathroom, I turned on the monitor (*Good! You can see the whole room still*); turned on the bath taps; then sat down on the toilet to wait.
Sitting in the bathroom, I heard the door open and Tosser entered.

"Are you ready for me, you cheeky little thing? Daddy's here!"
He saw the bed with the baby-doll nightie and looked across to the bathroom. He could hear the water running. Then he spotted the bottle of champagne with the two glasses and the card.

"Thoughtful little minx".
He poured himself a full glass and greedily guzzled it down. Then he topped up the glass for another.
"Don't be too long in there. I don't want to see you all crinkly".

He guzzled another glass, and refilled it once more.

Sitting down on the edge of the bed, he took another gulp, and put the glass down on the bedside table, kicking off his shoes. Then he shrugged off his jacket and threw it across at the chair next to the dressing table. He missed and the jacket slid off onto the floor.

I smiled "The wine is taking effect".

Tosser then laid back on the bed, stretching out his arms above his head.

After a few more minutes the sound of heavy, guttural snores started to rise up from the prone body.

"Ha! He's ready! You just wait here for a minute Flossie. I'll be back for you."

I then opened the door, cautiously approaching the sleeping Sergeant. He was well gone. My heart pounding in fear of him waking up (*what if I haven't used enough?*), I removed his trousers with shaking hands.

"Yeugh! I never want to ever think of doing this again. I'll be traumatised forever by the sight of Tosser's bare legs".

I folded the trousers and jacket, putting them in the back pack, along with the CCTV monitor and the covert camera (retrieved from its hiding place above the wardrobe).

Tosser was now lying flat out on the bed, wearing only his shirt, his tie pulled askew to one side; and a pair of baggy silk boxer shorts (in white, decorated with little red hearts). On his feet he wore his standard issue black socks, but bizarrely these were held up by a pair of black elastic suspenders around his calves (*Does anybody actually wear those things?*). He looked a ridiculous sight.

Crossing to the door, I looked out onto the corridor. All was clear. I had purposefully requested the room closest to the elevator. Crossing to the elevator, I pressed for it and waited. When it arrived, I placed the backpack in the entrance, preventing it closing and returning to another floor. Then returning to the room, I picked up the sleeping Sergeant, throwing his limp body over my shoulder and carried him to the elevator, laying him down inside.

Once more I returned to the room, crossing to the bathroom "Come on Flossie, we're ready for you now". Flossie was now fully prepared, the only thing she was wearing was a black leather collar, studded with diamantes, from which hung a matching lead, and of course an ample application of the bright red lipstick. I led her to the elevator and pushed her by the bottom inside with the sleeping Tosser.
I then opened the control panel to the lift and turned off the power. Finally I picked up the back pack and manually pushed the doors closed, apologising "Sorry Flossie, it won't be for long". As the doors closed I saw her big brown eyes looking up at me reproachfully, as she implored me:

"Baaaa!"

I then ran back down the back stairs, and out to the van in the rear alleyway and telephoned "999" for the emergency services.

A rather bored sounding voice answered "Emergency. What service do you require?"

Speaking in a falsetto voice, smiling to myself, I replied "I...I think it must be ..er .. the Fire...the lift is broken in the Grand Empire Hotel...on the High Street..erm..Westhaven. Please hurry! There's erm..er...somebody stuck in there...I can sort of, like hear somebody moving around in there, but they aren't answering me...They may be hurt...Perhaps you had better send the ambulance as well." I had to stop for a second to stifle a giggle, then finished "Please hurry!!"

As I finished the call I exploded into fits of laughter. My whole body shook and tears rolled down my cheeks. After a few minutes, with all of my stomach and ribs hurting, I managed to regain my composure. As I sat there in the van thinking of the sight of the sleeping Sergeant and his glamorous new lady friend, I could hear the sirens of the approaching emergency services. "I've got to see this!" Pulling on my best poker face, I got out of the van and walked slowly around to the front of the hotel, as though I had just finished on duty and was heading home.

At the front of the hotel I could see the fire engine and ambulance pulled up, parked askew on the pavement. The main crew had already gone inside, but one fireman was stood there for security, covering the rig. Crossing over to him, I made small talk, about what was the problem. "No I'm off duty now, thank goodness. Feel sorry for you lads though, having to be out on a cold night like this."

As we chatted, we saw the magnificent double polished mahogany doors of the prestigious hotel swing open. The first to emerge were the ambulance crew pushing a trolley bearing the sleeping sergeant, his dignity now covered by a pink fluffy blanket. Behind him then followed the fire crew, holding their sides and laughing; and at the rear came the head fireman leading Flossie the sheep by her diamante collar and lead.

Catching sight of me in uniform, he crossed over to me.

"Looks like one of your boys was doing a bit of entertaining," Unlike his colleagues, he was not laughing. In fact he was furious. "Stupid, perverted bastard! I just hope that we didn't have a real emergency while we were wasting our time with this clown. Bloody sergeant he is, too! Disgusting!"

Then handing me the lead, he added "And you can take care of his girlfriend here. We don't have facilities for these. I'll be writing to your Chief too, first thing in the morning. Have no doubt about that!"

Taking the lead, I watched as the two emergency vehicles pulled out, lights still flashing, but sirens now silent, and drove away into the night. Then, looking down at her, I smiled as I led her away back towards the van, "That's a really good girl, Flossie, you did an excellent job. Now let's wipe that lipstick off you and get you home. There'll be an extra special treat for you for supper."

After dropping Flossie off back at Hugh Johnson's farm, and thanking him, I called at the village lock up to collect the bicycle that I had been repairing during my evenings. I then drove to Luke Thompson's house, chaining the bike securely to the fence by his front door, using a new combination lock. I then wrote on a scrap of paper "The combination is 999" and dropped it through his letterbox.

Finally, I took Tosser's uniform back to the station and gave it to Helena to use it with Spanker in her next role playing session.

* * *

Spanker had collected the second body from the Station, as with Old Bob before him, wrapped in the king-sized satin sheets from Madam Sapphire's bed (although not this time quite so gently and lovingly), and was heading back with him to his undertaker's premises. He already had Old Bob there, laid out in his coffin, following his unexpected demise just the day before. Following the family's wishes, his coffin was still set up as an "open casket" in the "Chapel of Rest", but he was more than just a little bit bothered by that. Old Bob was just lying there smiling. It just didn't seem right.

I need to get rid of that smile.

He had told the family that he had died playing a game of golf. It had been the excitement, after all of these years, of getting a "hole in one". His son however, had been a bit surprised. He didn't even know that Bob played golf.

Musing to himself over his "new customer", presently stashed in the boot of his car, in his head he ran through his current "guests" awaiting interment:

Bob will be an open casket...cant use that one then.
Got a few other customers in:
One was an accident; a dog walker squashed by a block of falling blue ice from a passing Jumbo jet...'fraid that will have be a closed casket.

Another couple of them are Jewish, so they will be a speedy business – it will all have to be over in three days. They are ideal. They've already been viewed.

A few others have no relatives, they so won't be viewed either.

That Pimp is a big lad, so too much weight to hide in one coffin....need to spread the weight about a bit.

As he arrived back at his premises, he was thankful that he had waited a little until the evening light had begun to fade. It was almost dark as he turned into the private yard behind his Undertaker's parlour, pulling up next to the rear entrance, leading directly into the "Treatment Room". Opening the boot, he frowned down at the occupant.

He really is a big lad...going to have my work cut out lifting him on my own. At least at the Station I had the Ladies to help.

From inside the building he rolled out a long trolley bed, which had a cantilevered arm and a small hoist attached. Tying heavy-duty fabric straps around the cadaver, he hooked it up to the hoist. Then, with all strapping securely attached, he pressed the switch and an almost silent electric winch whirred to life, lifting the lifeless corpse out of the car boot and onto the stainless steel trolley.

Well that was money well spent. I knew it would come in handy one day...

Just a few minutes later he had the Illustrious Mr Lafitte lying on the stainless steel preparation table inside the clinically clean, white tiled Treatment Room, awaiting the final beauty treatment of his existence.

There was no way around it. He was going to have to saw him up. Then he would be able to put a little bit of him inside the coffins with each of his other "guests" when they make their final journey.

It won't do for the bits of him to leak out though – gonna have to wrap his parts in cling film...

Before he started though, he stood there scratching his head and trying to work out the calculations in his head. Maths was never really his forte.

It was going to be a bit of a problem. Him being a big lad was going make the five closed coffins that he had just identified, significantly heavier than expected.

An estimated 15 stone man, divided between 5 caskets would be 3 stone each.
That'll be too much...noticeable.

He had to revise his first estimations then:

I'll have to divide still further...will have to keep some back in freezer for next week and hope that no-one notices.

Then another solution came to him, drawing inspiration from the body of "Tyson", the pet corgi belonging to the squashed dog walker, who was currently still in the freezer awaiting collection. When they had first brought them into the mortuary, the two of them (both owner and his faithful hound) had been firmly compressed together by the solid mass of pungent blue ice mixed with excrement, and it had taken a couple of days before he had been able to even start the process of untangling the jumble of limbs.

I'll have to make the pieces small enough...wrap in black plastic, and label up as dog and two cats...I think "Samson", "Fluffy" and "Tiger" should do it.
Then, if anyone asks, I'm storing overflow for the vets.

Pulling on his bright yellow rubber galoshes and brilliant white waterproof (and blood-proof) coverall, protecting his face with a pair of goggles and face mask (to avoid breathing in the deadly bone dust) he set about the gruesome task of sawing up the body into more manageable sized pieces. Each piece was then securely wrapped in cling film, to guard against leakage. He then stashed just a couple of extra stone in each of the "intended to be closed" caskets, under each of the original occupants, disguising each parcel by slipping under the satin lining of the base, packing around with muslin cloth and sponge to prevent rolling.

Next, he cut a rough cardboard outline of the curled-up, sleeping shapes of the three imaginary deceased animals. Then, taking the final bundle of remaining "parcels", he arranged these to roughly resemble the outline of each cardboard animal, securing each by further layers of cling film wrapping. Finally each "Furry" bundle was wrapped in a thick, black bin-bag and a small white card attached to each, labelling them as "Samson", "Fluffy" and "Tiger" respectively. Standing back for a moment to admire his handiwork, he smiled to himself.

It is a very good job...impressive even. It is just a shame that nobody will ever get to see it.

Still smiling, he then placed his new furry "guests" in the freezer, alongside "Tyson", awaiting collection from the animal disposal van.

I'll just have to remember to use the trolley to move to and from the hearse. I can't let any of the pall bearers try carrying these. They would find the extra weight too suspicious. Especially Mrs Goldmeyer - she was only such a tiny little thing.

* * *

9 THE REVEREND

Reverend Ivor Goodfellow had been one of the best, most regular and devoted customers at "Blue" since its very first conception. You could say that he had attended almost "religiously". However, it had been a symbiotic relationship, beneficial to all parties. Not only had he benefitted from their regular "relaxation therapy massage" services, for which he had happily paid all disbursements, but his unrestricted use of the facilities had also afforded him free access to the CCTV control room. The Ladies had always been so very busy, being devoted to their work (which could be almost be described as being more of a vocation than a profession), that they had never noticed him slipping in to download the odd footage now and again. In fact it is probable that had they noticed him, they would have freely permitted him use of the recordings for his own personal enjoyment at home. Because of their generous natures, welcoming him into their "home", he felt no compunction in making use of the recordings for his own little business enterprise. God clearly provides him with every opportunity to raise church funds using any method that makes itself available. He was sure that God would approve whole heartedly of all of his hard work.

He knocked at the door of Councillor Roger's house, and was relieved when the door was answered by his wife, Chastity. He had been assured by Madame Sapphire that this would be an ideal time to visit Chastity (to ensure her "silence", to avoid her husband finding out about her involvement in "a few little matters"). The

Councillor was "guaranteed" not to be in, as he was always busy at his "therapy" sessions with Lady Helena at that time of day.

Unsuspecting of the motive for his visit, out of politeness, she invited the Reverend in for tea. As he sat in the comfort of her classically fashionable parlour, the inviting warmth of the open log fire, warmed his bones, and the tip of his chilled, red nose began to thaw out from its buffeting in this morning's frosty February weather outside. Today was not the warmest of days to have ventured out, and he was now regretting his choice of not having put on his heavy woollen overcoat over the top of his lightweight clerical suit, but he had set off out in too much haste. The chilled air of the winter season always tormented him, making his nose run constantly, obliging him to dab at it repeatedly with his crisp white linen handkerchief, occasionally dislodging his half lens "pins nez" glasses, secured to a cord around his neck. These he normally kept tucked into his small breast-side pocket when not in use, only being used for reading, but at this moment he had need of them to glance at the notes he had scribbled on a small piece of crumpled paper, and which he now retrieved from where it had been safely tucked inside his pocket-sized copy of the Bible.

Sipping at his cup of tea, he skirted around the true purpose of his visit, chattering on about the floral displays for the church (asking Chastity for her opinions in her capacity as leader of the Ladies Flower Arranging group), before eventually bringing the subject around to that of her marriage (twirling his glasses on their cords while deep in thought). He was, he advised her, deeply concerned.

A serious matter had been brought to his attention. It was a matter of the most delicate sensibilities. He barely knew how to bring himself to raise the matter. It was quite, quite shocking.

The suspense was killing her. She could not think what it might be. She wished that he would just hurry up and get to the point.

He asked whether they could use the TV. He felt that this was something that she needed to see, as he could bring himself to describe the true awfulness of it all.

She was now getting even more frustrated by his stalling.

Just get on with it man!

Seating themselves before the large plasma screen TV in Councillor Roger's lounge, the Reverend fumbled with the DVD casing, drawing out the agony, while he placed the disk into the machine. Then, sitting back in his seat with the controller in his hand, he continued "I apologise again, dear lady for the distress this is going to bring you. Are you sure that you want me to play this now. Or would you like me to come back later?"

Just get on with it! she screamed silently to herself.

He pressed the button and the machine whirred into action. The images formed on the huge screen, practically covering the lounge wall, almost like being in the front rows of a cinema. There before her were vivid and lurid images of herself indulging in rough and perverted sexual activities with an unknown man dressed in a studded latex suit, and who was wearing a tight-fitting, zipped leather mask over his face. The man appeared to be the passive recipient of her ministrations, and she the insatiable instigator of the events unfolding before her.

The Reverend then moved the images forward using the remote control to reveal a further "session": this time a threesome, with two entirely different persons: one a woman, and one a younger, slimmer, more athletic looking male, dressed in a "bondage" outfit of studded black leather strapping and tight black leather thong posing pouch.

Although she did not recognise any of the persons in the video, there was at the same time something disconcertingly familiar about them. She just could not place it. Similar in a way to how she had been struggling with herself all day to recall the events of yesterday. She could remember meeting Mrs Downey of the Ladies Flower Arranging Group in the morning, but the rest of the day was a blank.

"I am sure", the Reverend continued, "that like I, you would not want these sordid matters to reach your husband". "We must be most diligent to ensure that none of this reaches his attention. I assure you dear lady, I will be the absolute paragon of discretion in this matter. If at all possible, I shall make all endeavours to ensure that I do not have to place this recording in his possession. I am sure that you would be willing to work with me on this?"

Dumbfounded, she could not speak, only to nod in agreement.

"Then we shall say no more about this then. I would advise for you to keep quiet on all matters that may appear in any way contentious. Do not draw any further attention to yourself at all, and try to avoid involvement in anything at all political. Certainly, I should avoid your position as spokesperson for any of your action groups for a while, if I were you. I shall of course keep in touch, and am available at any time should you require my spiritual or moral guidance".

"Oh, I should also suggest that you ensure that your husband doesn't accidentally see that recording too," he added.

"I am sure that I can once more rely on your generosity to the church roof campaign, and your participation in our Garden Fete next month."

With that he rose and left.

* * *

10 THE COMMISSIONER'S VISIT

It was the morning after Lafitte had been here, trying to take over my business. We had all had a sleepless night, worrying about the recent turn of events. It had been several years since I set this business venture on its first teetering steps and lately things had been looking better and better. Business was doing well. Word of mouth had expanded our customer base without even any need for advertising. We had a good core group of reliable regular customers, all of whom were trustworthy. My girls could operate safely, securely and discretely. The only members of the public who knew about us were the ones who were important to us - our customers. Profits were up and we were now making a good contribution to the running of the station. As the cuts had started to bite at stations around the country, we had avoided it. We had safeguarded the pay and the jobs of those who were working here, and had not only been able to supplement everyday costs, like heating (the building was finally warm – no longer were we shivering in our outside coats, hugging hot water bottles) but we had even been able to pay for some of the much needed renovation costs. Even crime rates in the town had fallen dramatically (in fact it was almost non-existent), with practically no use being made of the cell facilities, apart from providing an overnight bed for the occasional drunk who had overindulged too much to go home.

Now in less than a week it was all going wrong. We had come to the attention of the big city pimps who wanted to muscle in on what they saw as a nice little earner and there had been two deaths in as many days. Although we appeared to have successfully covered these up, at least for now anyway, it was worrying to say the least.

On top of that the very existence of the station was at risk. The new commissioner was due to visit any day. Word had it that he was looking to close us down, transferring us off to larger city branches, because on paper we had that almost non-existent crime rate. If we had no crime, we didn't need a station. They didn't realise (and we certainly couldn't tell them) that the reason there was no crime was because we were so successful at what we did. Shut us down and the crime would come back in spade-fulls.

Then came the final straw! That useless tosser of a Sergeant had 'phoned in this morning. He was unable to come to work as he was feeling sick, so we were a man down. Funnily enough, Tim didn't seem too surprised. I wasn't sure quite what he knew, or what he had been up to, but I'd swear I heard him mutter "I'll bet his is. I just wonder if it's the after effects of the drugged wine, or if it is just that he can't show his face for the shame of where he was found." When I asked him to explain he just said it was better if I didn't know anything about it.

At the same time that the Reverend had been conducting his "visit" to Chastity, her husband was, as was the case on every other morning, engaging in his favourite pastime at "Blue. On that morning, Tim and I had been in the CCTV room. He had come to me that morning with some idea he had which he said may help the crime statistics. He started by outlining how our current activities were funding the Police station and keeping down crime, but that was then causing our problem, as Head Office were using that criteria to say that the station was no longer needed. We needed to increase the crime rate, on paper but without destroying all of our good work by increasing it for real. All of the new "crimes" would need to be verifiable: we would need to be able to identify the culprit, so we couldn't just invent bogus people. We would need real people, and he thought that he had found a way to do it.

It was intriguing. If his idea worked we would have a solution to one of the main problems endangering the station, so we were busily chatting at the same time that we had been reviewing the CCTV monitoring of the dungeon activities, our attention not fully on the job before us. Firstly, however he pressed the arrow button on the machine to select the cameras covering the Black room, to check on Spanker and Lady Helena preparing for their usual, daily session. This time, Spanker was dressed in a police officer's jacket, loosely covering a black wet-look lycra thong; with a black leather restraining harness, crossing his centre chest. A leather "gimp" mask covering his entire face, save for three round holes for eyes and mouth, fastened tightly to the contours of his head, closed by a zip passing from the centre forehead to the nape of the neck. All seemed fine in there, so we moved on to the next room. Barely waiting for more than a second or two, he then pressed the arrow button once more, revealing the Red Room, where we saw one of our most prestigious customers, a High Court Judge, busy "in session" with Sabrina, who was today providing her alternate role as a fantasy fairy-story submissive. The bed was now covered in white satin sheets, and soft, classical music could be heard playing in the background.

The Judge was seated in the Queening chair (its central hole now covered by a board and an upholstered cushion), still wearing his Judge's gown, straight from completing a session in the neighbouring Assizes. Sabrina was dressed as Goldilocks, and was play acting out the part of being accused of "breaking and entering" into Mr Bruin Bear's home; and the "theft" of food (having allegedly eaten some of both Mr and Mrs Bear's breakfast, and also all of their young son, Bruin Bear Junior's porridge). As she knelt in front of him, the Judge strutted back and forth in front of the suppliant and submissive Goldilocks telling her that she had been a very naughty girl and would need to be punished.

He then ordered her to strip off her panties. She complied coyly, faking embarrassment, and offered them to him. He then took the offered undergarment, sniffed it, licked it and tucked it into his jacket pocket. Ordering her to bend over the leather bench, grasping the bottom of the bench legs, and spreading her legs, he then lifted the hem of her skirt and flounced petticoats, raising them over her head to expose her full, rounded buttocks and rosy red cheeks. Suddenly, he thrust a finger forcefully into her exposed anus, making her gasp and cry out loudly in both pain and pleasure, as he rotated and probed her in a circular motion. He then withdrew from her slowly, trailing his finger down through the blossoming rosy lips of her labia to the raised button of her engorged clitoris, massaging as she arched her back and groaned with the effort to restrain herself. Then he plunged two fingers deep down inside her, while still continuing his relentless massaging of her button. Her head jerked back, her eyes wide, her mouth open and gasping. Her back arched deeper, her knuckles white as she gripped at the legs of the bench, while he bent forward and slowly licked the full length of her sex, from the back to the front button of her clitoris.

Tim was just about to explain how we could find these "real people" willing to take on bogus crimes for our statistics when at that very moment my mobile vibrated, where I had it tucked into one of the few possible places in my costume – in the elasticated garter on my left thigh. Looking at the text message coming through on the 'phone, it was an alert to warn us that the Commissioner was on his way today. In fact he would be arriving within the next twenty minutes. Our discussion would have to wait. There was much yet to be done and little time in which to do it. Both of the girls were "tied up" with their work (possibly literally by now), so there was only the two of us to stash any incriminating equipment that should not be lying around.

It was just then that things went from bad to worse, and everything got even more complicated. As we were tidying the Common Room, the internal telephone went off. This time it was the officer on counter duty, with the message that we had two more visitors, and they had put one in each of the two front interview rooms...

Two!! What on earth had we done to deserve this?

One visitor was Colin Sniffer, a hack from the local newspaper. He was stupid but dangerous. He had come about the Commissioner's intended visit and had also heard about Chastity's campaign against

98

sleaze. He was trying to get a story, but even if there wasn't one, he wasn't opposed to making one up.

We would desperately have to keep him away from both the Judge and Spanker; and prevent him from seeing any of the equipment. I could leave him in the interview room for a few minutes, but would have to let him out soon or he would get suspicious.

Our other guest was Chastity. The Counter officer had said that she was apparently quite agitated, so he had given her a cup of tea, but suggested we deal with her quickly "before she loses it altogether".

That doesn't sound good either!

I found myself thinking aloud as I tried to think out a plan (or at least some kind of structured panic anyway):

"Not good Tim. We've got a two pronged attack. We've still got Spanker in there with Lady Helena and we need to keep Chastity away from there. She can't find him here. We've also got to keep that reporter, Sniffer away from everybody, and make sure he sees nothing at all. We can let him see as much as the Commissioner, but that's just about nothing of any importance. I reckon that we should give the reporter a cup of tea and get him to sit quiet until the Commissioner arrives, then take them both on a tour together. In the meantime, I can get Chastity out of the way and into my room for a chat, while you warn Helena and get Spanker out of here. Then, when the Commissioner arrives, whichever of us is free will start the tour, and the other will join it as soon as possible. So first things first, you see to Sniffer and I'll get Chastity."

Tim then set off to Interview Room 2 with a cup of tea for Sniffer and I headed for Room 1 for Chastity, opening the door with my most welcoming smile. "Mrs Robinson-Rogers, what a lovely surprise to see you again so soon. Won't you join me in my room, then you can tell me all about it." So, it was with a very strange feeling in the pit of my stomach that I sat down in my office, face to face with Chastity, both of us drinking a very civilized cup of tea, especially when I thought back to the very entertaining afternoon we had spent with her just yesterday. But Chastity didn't seem to recognise me, other than as the Harriet Harrison she had met at the Station previously. She seemed just to be interested in back tracking her activities of the day before. She could not seem to remember where she had been, or what she had been doing in the afternoon. Our little group "session" seemed to have been forgotten, now just a distant memory of a series of erotic dreams that she didn't want to admit to. She certainly didn't seem to have recognised me or Tim from the Reverend's video show. She clearly must have thought that it had happened somewhere else, perhaps where she had visited later. She did tell me though that she was worried that she may have either had some kind of seizure and imagined a most lurid waking nightmare, or that she may have been drugged and abducted.

I laughed "Chastity my dear, abductions here, in Westhaven of all places? Nothing ever happens here any more exciting than perhaps somebody accidentally putting a foreign coin in the Reverend's collection dish. She smiled, then laughed along with me "You're right of course. Who on earth would want to abduct the Chair of the Flower Arranging Group?" Then a serious expression passed over her face. "But then Miss Harrison, does that mean that I am going mad? Did I imagine it?"

"Oh no! I'm sure not. It was probably just something you ate. You must have just have had a tummy upset. You did eat rather a lot of those little cakes yesterday, you know."

"Oh how embarrassing! I do hope you don't think too badly of me. Was I a real glutton then? I do apologise. I vaguely remember that they were very tasty." Then she added, "I don't suppose you have any more?"

Just at that moment, my mobile erupted into action, vibrating against my leg where I had it safely tucked behind my garter belt. Quickly retrieving it, unseen by Chastity, I glanced at the screen.

Damn! The Commissioner has arrived!

I'm terribly sorry, Chastity but something has just come up. I'm afraid I'm going to have to leave you for a few minutes, but please, do make yourself at home. Help yourself to some more tea...oh, and do have a few more cakes if you really did enjoy them so much." Then lifting out a bowl of cakes from my desk drawer, I made my hasty escape off towards the front counter to greet the Commissioner.

I hope she behaves herself while I'm gone...

* * *

Meanwhile, at Sapphire's suggestion, Tim had taken a mug of tea into Interview Room 2 for Colin Sniffer, the reporter. The newspaper hack was a shabby little man, wearing a tattered old mackintosh, with a pair of battered and worn brown leather shoes on his feet. Slung around his neck he carried his "badge of office", his black leather camera case.

"I thought you might like another cuppa" Tim offered, as he handed him the mug of steaming milky tea. "We have had word that the Commissioner is on his way at this very moment and will be having a tour of the Station. Miss Harrison thought that you might want to accompany him, perhaps taking a few shots to cover the story for your paper? We aren't sure how far away he is at the moment, but he shouldn't be long. Make yourself comfortable in the meantime."

"How thoughtful. Thank you" he responded, gratefully taking the offered beverage and sitting himself down at the desk.

Mission 1 accomplished Tim thought to himself, with a smile at how easily that had gone, then turned to leave through the door into the main corridor.

Now for Spanker!

Sniffer looked up through the steam of his tea. That young copper was a bit too quick to fob him off there, he thought to himself. He couldn't wait to get out of here too! I'm pretty sure he forgot to lock that door after him too. Maybe it wouldn't hurt just to have a little look around before the Commissioner gets here..." Setting down his mug on the table and picking up his camera he slipped quietly out through the door into the corridor behind Tim.

Sniffer watched Tim as he hurried down the corridor to one of the cell doors. This was the Black Room, Lady Helen's dungeon. Pressing on the buzzer switch to the side of the door, Tim activated the interior alarm, setting off a continuous low hum, and triggering a steady flashing of the room up-lighters, now illuminated in a soft red glow. Almost immediately the door opened by a narrow crack and a worried looking Lady Helena appeared. Tim explained to her that the Commissioner was due any minute and that Chastity was already in the building. She had to evacuate her "guest" immediately.

At that, the door opened fully and Lady Helena emerged into the corridor, fastening a kimono-type robe around her, tying it shut with a sash at her waist. Waving her hand behind her for her "guest" to follow, she was then followed out by a male wearing a black leather and lycra bondage outfit and matching full-face gimp mask. Over the top of his outfit he was wearing a Police Sergeant's jacket, bearing the numbers 7865, the trousers to complete the uniform rolled up under his arm. The three of them then headed further along the passageway until they reached a door marked "Toilets". They entered furtively and crossed to the window.

As Sniffer watched them unseen from the corridor, Tim and Lady Helena assisted their "guest" as he made his escape through the toilet window, and made his way off across the gardens behind the station, jumping the low picket fences wearing only his gimp costume, with the sergeant's uniform loosely thrown over the top, and still clutching the trousers under his arm. His face was too obscured by the gimp mask for Sniffer to be able to recognise him, but the number 7865 on the jacket, and the stripes on the arms, clearly identified him as "Sergeant 7865 Archibald Toscer." Quickly exiting the building by the rear door, Sniffer set off across the gardens in pursuit, his black leather camera case slung around his neck, but with his camera now grasped firmly in his hand, trying to get pictures "for a scoop".

Tim watched him with a smile as he vaulted the picket fences, following the trail of his quarry. That was a sight you don't see every day.

Then he too turned away and headed for the counter to greet the Commissioner.

* * *

Police Commissioner, Gordon Gordon had arrived and was waiting impatiently at the front counter. He was not exactly what Tim had been expecting to see. Rather than an imposing man with the power to control every Police Station in the region, the man before him was wearing an ill-fitting, shiny, food-stained grey suit, and the biggest "faux pas" for any well-dressed gentleman, brown shoes! He appeared to be somewhere in his mid-fifties, short, fat and bald, with round wire-rimmed glasses covering his blue-grey eyes.

Trying to put on his most polite and respectful voice, Tim greeted him with a smile, ignoring the scowl that answered him in return, and invited the Commissioner to join him on a tour of the Station. "Miss Harrington", he advised, would be joining them imminently, but had been unavoidably detained.

Chastity meanwhile, had not remained in Sapphire's office, but had followed her out into the corridor. As she passed the door to the CCTV control room however, she had glanced inside, her attention drawn to the scene being played out on one of the monitors. She was sure that she had seen her husband, "Spanker" (despite the figure that she had seen wearing some kind of mask), and puzzled as to what he was doing there, and more importantly why he was wearing that outlandish costume, she was determined to find out!

The Commissioner however, had set off on his "guided tour" with Tim, and was being shown around the station when he saw Chastity hurrying towards the cells to confront her errant husband. Intrigued as to what she was doing, he followed her, insisting on going a different way than his guide, Tim, had intended.

Just ahead of him, Chastity burst through the door to the Red room in error, closely followed by the Commissioner, both of them standing frozen – transfixed by the scene before them of the Judge "in session" with Lady Sabrina.

The Judge was once more seated in the Queening chair, still wearing his Judge's gown, with Sabrina, dressed as "Goldilocks", kneeling between his legs. He commanded her "As you are such a greedy girl, always hungry and never satisfied, I think I will fill you up properly," pointing to his manhood. She reached up and unfastened the front of his silk breeches, allowing his engorged shaft to burst free. Raising herself slightly on her knees, she leant forward, trailing her tongue the full extent of his length, from the junction with his scrotum to the tip of his helmet, swirling the tip of her tongue around the rim of his retracted foreskin and over the shiny globe of its swollen head. Then parting her lips as wide as she could stretch, she engulfed his shaft with her mouth, sinking it deep down into the back of her throat.

As Chastity and the Commissioner stood silently in the doorway, Madame Sapphire followed them in through the door, her face breaking into a broad smile as she immediately recognised the Commissioner's shocked and horrified face as that of a customer and old flame from many years before.

"Pee Wee! Fancy meeting you here after all these years!" she squealed, reaching up on the tips of her toes, throwing her arms, around his neck and planting on his lips the most familiar and demonstrative kiss that Chastity had ever seen, one leg raising to wrap around his body as she ground her hips into his. She was sure that her tongue must have reached halfway to his navel. That kiss just did not seem physically possible.

* * *

11 A NEW VOCATION

It was the morning after the Commissioner's visit and I have to admit, I had had barely a wink of sleep last night. Finally it was all over. Whatever we had feared would happen had happened, and whatever was to come of it all, there was no undoing it all now. The uncertainty of that outcome still hung over us though, and the trepidation of knowing how it would all play out was eating away at the pit of my stomach. All of those months of preparation: of hiding equipment so that the Commissioner would not see it and suspect; the manipulation of political opponents, particularly the corruption and blackmail of Chastity (despite that she appeared to have fully enjoyed it), and elimination of business rivals (thankfully, that was one secret that hadn't got out – let's hope it stays that way) – all had come to a head yesterday and now the Commissioner knew everything (well, almost everything).

Who would have thought it though, that Police Commissioner Gordon Gordon would've turned out to be none other than my little "Pee Wee". If I had known it was him, I never would have bothered with all of this rigmarole of squirreling away the evidence.

I sat in the quiet privacy of my office, with my steaming mug of latté while I mused over "Life, the Universe and Everything". My "Pee Wee", the Police Commissioner!. How he had changed though since the days when we were both undergrad Law students, way back in the distant swirling mists of our youth. We had been inseparable then. We had even thought of moving in together, with that twinkling little fantasy of the "Happy ever After", with a pretty little house and 2.4 children playing in the garden. It just wasn't to be though. I wouldn't make that jump, frightened of committing to a long-term relationship, and terrified of taking our "friendship" to that next level. I had been "saving myself" for the right man, and couldn't be sure that he was the one. At least that is, not until he was gone! Because, then of course we graduated, and he got an offer to work for a big Corporation overseas. It was too good to turn down. He had begged me to go with him, but I was too "chicken".

After he was gone though, I had realised what I had done: how I had missed my opportunity though misguided morality. So, I made a decision and changed! From that point on, I was no longer the meek little girl who was too frightened to take a chance. If I saw an opportunity, I grasped it with both hands. If an idea flashed into my head, I followed it, milking every drop of opportunity from it. I was now much stronger, shying away from nothing. Some may even say I was cold and calculating.

I realised then, that it wasn't just him. We had both changed.

But yesterday, it was almost as though we had never been apart. We fitted back together like missing pieces from a puzzle: only now we both had grown. Our experience and self-confidence allowed us to take our relationship far beyond that barb-wired boundary of morality.

After everyone had burst in through that door into Lady Helena's dungeon all thoughts of secrecy evaporated. She had however, managed to convince the Judge that it was all part of the service – that the public humiliation of being found out in the middle of his perverse debauchery was deliberate. She was punishing him with the ultimate torture – that of being "caught in the act". Then she gave him an extra thrashing for "being a dirty little pervert!" After that he loved every minute of it. He even paid her an extra bonus – said it was the best session he had ever had.

Priceless!!

Chastity had rather surprised me too. The sight of the dungeon, with the oversized leather bed and all of its special "toys" suspended from the walls; along with the heady aromas of essential oils and beeswax leather polish, had brought back the lost memories of her earlier visit. I have to admit even I had been shocked when she had turned seductively to poor little Tim, grasping him by the tie, and dragged him off into the Black Room.

It's a damn good job I had all of that extra soundproofing put in last year...

I was just smiling to myself, through the foggy haze of my hot latté, thinking about young Tim (how much he had helped us out this last few days; how much of a team member he had become in such a short time; wondering whether he could even walk straight this morning...), when as if by planned co-incidence he knocked at my open door.

"Got a minute, Harry? I never got around to finishing our little chat yesterday..."

"Sure. Come in and grab a brew."

He slipped in through the door, closing it behind him to ensure that nobody could overhear our conversation. As he helped himself to a mug of coffee and made himself comfortable in the only other serviceable chair in my tiny office, I couldn't help noticing how nicely that shapeless mess of a Police uniform hung off his figure: his slim but muscular frame, his narrow hips, the not inconsiderable bulge at the front...

Stop it girl! Are you insatiable? Do you never stop thinking about sex?

To begin with though I wanted to tell him of another strange thing, although I was sure he had a hand in it somehow:
"This morning there has been an irate call from the Chief at HQ. He has had his ear burned off by the Chief Fire Officer about

wasted time, endangering the public, hoax calls etc. Apparently one of our officers (quite a senior one actually) had been found in a drunken state of undress, having intimate relations with an animal (namely a sheep) in a public place. Our Chief had covered it up but was demanding the person concerned should resign. Don't suppose you know anything about it do you Tim?"

He shook his head, but looked furtively down towards his shoes, fidgeting with his toes.

I continued: "He has even emailed through to me a photograph of the perpetrator! Then, as if that weren't enough, I had also been contacted by Colin Sniffer, the journalist who was here yesterday. He claims to have taken a photograph of a person wearing an "obscene outfit", under a Police officer's uniform, jumping around the neighbouring gardens. He couldn't identify the person involved as he had been wearing one of those leather gimp masks, but the uniform had sergeant's stripes and carried the number 7865. I'm sure you are aware that this would clearly identify him as "Sergeant Archibald Toscer".

He spluttered a little into his coffee, but I was sure that I could detect a smile on his lips, even hidden behind the cup and its steamy contents.

"It may come as no surprise to you to hear then that, sadly we have also heard this morning that Sergeant Toscer has had to resign on grounds of ill health, with effect immediately. He will however, be unable to come back in to collect his personal belongings as he has been Sectioned by the Police doctor and admitted to Westhaven Psychiatric Hospital, and is expected to be there for the foreseeable future. Perhaps you could do me the favour of clearing his locker into a storage box? You can put it in one of the lock-ups until we can figure out what to do with it."

* * *

So with that bit of housekeeping out of the way, Tim had his chance to finish telling me his idea for how we could increase the crime rate statistics:

As he had begun yesterday, he set out how our current activities were funding the Police station and keeping down crime, but that this falling crime rate was self defeating, as Head Office uses that criteria to decide whether the station is no longer needed. We needed some way of increasing numerically our crime statistics without actually increasing real crime.

He continued by showing how all crimes listed in the statistics need to be verifiable: they need to identify the culprit, so we can't just invent bogus people. We need real people. However, we cannot just list fake offences against real people as, even if we paid their fines through "Blue's" profits, the individuals named would get a Police record that may come to light in future criminal record checks. So, we need to have convictions that don't carry fines and don't leave a trail.

Ok so far - sounds fine in theory, but not easy to do in practice...

His idea was then to write up bogus crimes, drawn at random from a list of possible minor infractions, using recently deceased people as perpetrators. They would never complain, and they would never need to ask for a CRB (a listing of the Police computer record of their convictions). Furthermore, if we only give these people "cautions" (where a person admits guilt without making a court appearance), they will count as a "conviction" but without there being any record of a court hearing.

However, in order for this to work, the "accused" would need to give their fingerprints and be photographed for their Police files.

This was where Spanker came in. Apparently he had been chatting with him and it turns out that he holds a contract with the Council to supply funerals for all of those deceased without families, or who are insolvent. Their actual, physical bodies will be at his premises. He can provide names, addresses, dates of birth and National Insurance numbers for each of them. He can then take fingerprints and take photographs of the culprits (he can pose the deceased in a similar way to what the Victorians used to do with their loved ones, to make them appear as though they were still alive).

Then Tim said that he would be able to write up the crimes "creatively", with dates for their "offences" taking place prior to the dates of their deaths, so appearing to have happened while the perpetrators were still alive. He could then produce a full prosecution file, but instead to following it to a full "conviction", he would close it off with a "caution", so avoiding any court appearances.

That way we would get to increase the crime rate, without actually hurting anybody. The perpetrators will never know because they are dead (so they aren't bothered about their reputations), and will never apply for passports, visas or anything else requiring a CRB check. Nobody would ever know a thing.

He had already discussed it with Spanker and had identified a number of "offenders" for the previous quarter to start with. He added that we would have to start slow though, as it would look suspicious to have a crime rate that spontaneously shoots up for no apparent good reason.

It was a truly brilliant suggestion!

Now all we would have to worry about would be the Commissioner closing them down (although I was sure that "Little Pee Wee" would not be any great problem), and a tiny little matter of a murder and a manslaughter that are best not mentioned to anyone...

I was right though earlier. That boy had definitely made himself an essential member of our team. We would need to reward him for all of his hard work...

* * *

Pleased with how well Madame Sapphire seemed to have taken up his suggested solution to their statistics problem, Tim hurried off to the Common Room. Bursting with pride and excitement, he could hardly wait to tell the girls (especially Lady Sabrina) that she had now promoted him - making him a full member of the "family": still acting as doorman/security, but also now acting as occasional "Bondage Master". His new BDSM name was to be "Master Justin Trousersnake".

He hoped that Sabrina would be pleased with him. She had been "off" with him since the other day when he had gone with Lady Helena for his "Taster session". She hadn't understood how he saw her as purity itself. When the opportunity had presented itself, he could not bring himself to choose her. It was because he was so naïve and in-experienced that he did not want her to see him as a fumbling idiot. He had wanted to worship her as a goddess: to wrap her in silk and keep her pure, away from all things unclean. He wanted to take her out to dinner, for wine and a candle-lit meal. He wanted her as his girlfriend – not to be her customer!

Now when he opened the Common Room door, his stomach turned somersaults and the excited little man in his head, who had been bouncing to tell everyone his news, was now strangely silenced. He imagined him bound to a chair by red chiffon ties, his mouth gagged with a black leather bridle bit between his teeth. He was on his own! What was he going to say to her?

He need not have worried. As she saw him frozen in the doorway, the expression on his terrified face looking exactly like a "bunny in the headlights", Lady Sabrina broke into a wide smile. Rushing to him and grasping both of his hands tightly, she looked up into his eyes and told him how she was very proud of the way he had helped to save them all, especially what he had done about Tosser. She was sorry that she had been angry with him and wanted to make it up to him (but she did add that it was on condition that he no longer visited Lady Helena for any pre-marital "therapy sessions", but come to her instead."

"Pre-marital therapy sessions" she said – that sounded like she wants this to get serious... Very serious...

Tim beamed at the thought of "Pre-marital therapy sessions" with Lady Sabrina. He realised that he was not the same innocent boy that he had been when he had put his foot right in it and refused her earlier. Now he was only too happy to take up her offer...

"There is no time like the present", Sabrina purred at him suggestively, intending that they start on his training right now. Taking him by the hand she led him out into the corridor and up a narrow stairway at the end. He had wondered what that door was for, but had never gotten around to asking. At the top of the stairs, he saw a door, marked "Archives". This was a room where he had never been before. It had not appeared on any of the usual CCTV control menus. Apparently it was normally a hidden camera, only activated on rare occasions when the room was in use.

As the door opened he was taken in by the beauty of its decoration. This was the "Pink Room", only usually used for personal matters, occasional "vanilla" or fairy story fantasies. Despite its name, the room was mostly gleaming white: its ceiling, its deep shag pile carpeting and the softly flocked wallpaper, the latter in white interspersed with tiny pink flowers. In the centre of the room was a king-sized four-poster bed, elaborately carved in mahogany, covered with white satin sheets; and long pink chiffon curtains flowed from the top of each of the four bed posts.

It was like stepping into a fairy story.

"Do you like ice-cream Tim?" she asked innocently.
"Yes..?" he answered hesitatingly, unsure of what she had planned.
"Good! Because you are about to get the best "Vanilla" you ever tasted!" dragging him gently through the door of the Pink Room

* * *

Later that afternoon, Police Commissioner Gordon Gordon, otherwise forever to be known by his alias of "Pee Wee", had arrived once more (although no longer on official business), and was in the Blue room enjoying an afternoon of reminiscing with Madame Sapphire over a bottle of the best red wine from her private cellar.

She had explained to him their planned increase to the crime rate, as a solution to their imminent threat of closure, and he was sure that he would be able to "wangle" it by the politicians, as justification to leave them to continue their work as they had always done. In addition, he had been thinking up a few plans of his own. Impressed with the way that they had turned around the flailing finances of the Station, and how they had cut the local crime rate to virtually zero (ignoring of course their now intended bogus crime wave), he suggested that rather than curtail activities, they should look to expansion.

He proposed that between them they should open a new branch in the next town, suggesting that they take over the Probation Service offices as an ideal location (in his view, the brothel would prevent more re-offenders than the Probation Officers ever could). The only real problem would be as to who would run it. Madame Sapphire had her hands full (literally sometimes) in running the Westhaven-on-Sea branch. She could not be expected to run a second set of dungeons as well.

Sapphire however, thought that she may have the ideal candidate, leading him to the doorway. Spanker had just arrived for his usual session. However, instead of sending him to Lady Helena as usual, he was directed to a new masked dominatrix, Lady Whiplash.

It was Chastity!

She had now discovered her true calling as a Dominatrix and had joined the team. She had also just discovered her husband's penchant for being a Submissive; how he had deceived her for all of these years into thinking that he was not interested in sex; and how she had repressed her own highly demanding sexual needs in order to survive the virtual "desert" in which she had found herself existing. But no more...

At the sound of her voice, Spanker had scurried away terrified, but there was no escape, and Chastity found Spanker cowering behind a filing cabinet in the corridor.

"Get here boy! You have a lot to answer for."

At that she reached out and grabbed him by the back of his collar, dragging him off into the Black room for his punishment.

Commissioner Gordon chuckled as the helpless Spanker was hauled away for a severe disciplining by his wife, remarking, "Now, I like her. She's got real potential!"

Sapphire laughed, "Commissioner, may I introduce you to the Madam in charge of your new city branch, Lady Whiplash!"

* * *

ABOUT THE AUTHOR

The author, writing under a pseudonym, is a best-selling author of non-fiction academic books, currently dipping a toe into different genres (this time of adult fiction), to see how the other half live.

I am married, the mother of 4 grown up children, and a hairy herd of four-legged love sponges. By buying this book you help to supplement the ever growing waistline of the greediest spaniel on the planet and her entourage - an ever-increasing collection of toothless, geriatric cats. You can get in touch with me through my Facebook page:
Willow Birch

Although you will have no doubt found this work listed under the genre of erotic fiction, it is equally very much a Black Comedy, although a little naughty, and I would hope that it leaves you more with a giggle than a thrill.

Printed in Great Britain
by Amazon